Flowering Thorn

Flowering Thorn

MARY WILLIAMS

ROBERT HALE · LONDON

© Mary Williams 1997
First published in Great Britain 1997

ISBN 0 7090 5996 5

Robert Hale Limited
Clerkenwell House
Clerkenwell Green
London EC1R 0HT

Photoset in North Wales by
Derek Doyle & Associates, Mold, Clwyd.
Printed in Great Britain by
St Edmundsbury Press Ltd, Bury St Edmunds, Suffolk.
Bound by WBC Book Manufacturers Limited,
Bridgend, Mid-Glamorgan.

1

1856

The lonely scene was like the imprint of a mirage on the mind.

I was walking along a deserted road through a grey light that could have been morning or evening. I had no idea of my identity or where I was going. Everything around me had the unreal quality of a dream. On one side rough moorland rose upwards to the lowering sky; on the other the land fell abruptly to the glassy darkness of a motionless sea. Far ahead the crouched hills loomed in monstrous toadstool shapes against a silvered cold background.

Everywhere was very quiet. No sign of any human thing or animal to break the unearthly silence; only the monotonous soft tread of my own feet as they followed the winding track. I had no thoughts or feelings – only an automatic sense of destiny that drew me inevitably to some mysterious conclusion.

And then, round an unexpected bend of the lane, there rose the silhouetted dark shape of a house projecting sentinel-like from the sea side of the landscape. There was nothing beautiful about it, but something – some unknown magnetic force – impelled me ahead and quickened my footsteps. The damp air brushed the tumbled hair from my face and my sight clarified.

As I neared the great iron gates a feeling of familiarity filled me, though I had no conscious memory of having been there before. They were slightly open, and I went through along a paved path leading to an arched porch. On either side macabre carved gargoyles stared down on me. It was as though they waited to herald my return from a long journey.

I mounted the steps, and pushed the iron door. It opened with a grating sound. As I went in dank air seemed to solidify and encompass me.

It was then that I fell.

I regained consciousness to find myself lying on a narrow bed in a badly lit room encumbered by heavy furniture. A thin greyish light suggesting it was early morning streamed from a narrow window through heavy lace curtains, emphasizing an atmosphere of bleak unfriendliness. I felt stiff, and my head ached; when I touched my jaw there was the rough impact of what felt like mud or dried blood.

I sat up and there was a wrench of pain in my foot. I tried to think back but could remember nothing except the darkness and the fall. Obviously someone must have undressed me. I was wearing a coarse cotton garment – a nightdress presumably – buttoned at the neck.

Where was I? *Who*? And how had I got there?

The confusion of questions was throbbing through my mind when a door at my right grated open and a woman came in. She was tall and broad, wearing a black dress, with a shred of lace perched on the top of her piled-up mass of ginger hair. Her eyes were small and black and penetrating, and I caught a whiff of gin on her breath when she spoke.

'Feeling better now?'

'No,' I answered truthfully. 'What happened? Where am I?'

She poked her head forward. 'Don't you remember? Your name? Nothing?'

'Not anything. No. Not even my name. Except—' I broke off trying desperately to picture some meaning to the sensation of mystery and terror that had driven me there.

'Yes? Except—?' The jarring voice was insistent.

'Nothing. Just *nothing*. Tell me, *please*. For heaven's sake—'

'Don't swear, girl. We have no swearing in Master Silas Trevanion's house. You just mind your manners and show proper respect to those in charge. And that includes me. I'm Mistress Susannah, sister to Master Silas, and his housekeeper. Through Mr Justin Llarne I've been given care of you until you've recovered from your accident. So

just see you remember it and no tantrums or disobedience, mind.'

'Tantrums?' I gasped. 'Disobedience? What do you
mean? What are you to me? Or – or Master Silas? And Mr
Llarne? Who's Mr Llarne?'

She gave a short harsh laugh. 'Ha! Someone you wanted
to forget, no doubt.' The large chin took an extra forward
thrust; I could see the hairs on it. 'Your name is Jane. Mr
Justin, my girl, is your husband, and a pretty dance you've
led him these last days. If you hadn't gone walking where
you'd no right, strictly against his orders, you wouldn't be
in such a plight now. Had a fall you did, on the rocks. No
wonder your head aches. Concussion all right, and on top
of that illness you'd had. He should have taught you
obedience earlier in a man's way – that would have saved
us all a deal of trouble.' She paused for a moment before
continuing, 'Well, I'll waste no more breath now. There's
plenty to do here, and I've Master Silas's breakfast to get.
Yours'll come later. He always needs a good meal before
going to chapel. An' today's Sunday. He's a sermon to
deliver.' Her lips tightened in a smug self-satisfied line. 'A
lay preacher he is,' she added, 'and very respected by the
village. You'll meet him when he gets back. Maybe a sight
of him'll jog your memory. They say a glimpse of one of
God's chosen can do a deal to banish the bad things.'

'Oh.' I could think of nothing more to say.

She gave a little jerk of the head and glanced at what
appeared to be a seaman's chest in one corner.

'There are clothes ready in there – petticoats and what a
modest woman needs, with a dress, all neat and tidy, and
far more respectable than that frilly thing you was

wearing. You c'n have a wash now before I bring food up, and prepare yourself to face my brother and Mr Justin. You'll find water there for washing and a bar of soap.' She indicated a large ewer and basin on an old-fashioned deal washstand, then left abruptly snapping the door to with a sharp click. There was a further grating of a key being turned, and despite my throbbing head, resentment filled me with renewed anger. I got up and limped across the floor to try the knob. As I thought there was no response.

I was locked in.

A prisoner.

Why?

And *where?*

If I could only remember *one thing* – had a single clue of my identity, and what had driven me to such a place, circumstances would not have been so terrifying. But there was nothing. Only the explanation given by that ugly, domineering woman who'd treated me like a naughty child and informed me I had a husband, Mr Justin Something-or-other – Llarne, that was the name – who'd put me in her charge. I couldn't accept it, and yet I had a gold ring on the third finger of my left hand, and I'd obviously been in some accident that had impaired my memory. Concussion she'd said. Well, if it was that I'd recover it some time and remember. I was bound to, surely? – or *would* I?

In a wave of desperation I crossed to the narrow window facing the bed from the far wall and looked out.

A thin watery sun was creeping above the distant rim of sea and sky, sending a zig-zagging pathway of quivering light over the ruffled water. On my left a humped line of rounded hills rose from the jagged cliffs. Pulling the curtains further aside I glanced down. The house I was in appeared from the view I had, to be very near the cliff edge. There was the thud of waves breaking, and a sudden gust of wind blew a shower of sand against the window panes, temporarily obscuring the panorama. I closed my eyes and tried to think, in an effort somehow to bridge the darkness of lost memory.

It was no use. The nightmare persisted.

The driven sand itself was like a veil obscuring reason – an elemental force conjured up by some power to defeat normality.

I started shivering, and for moments could not stop. When at last I got my nerves under control the outside air had cleared a little but the promise of sunshine ahead had gone leaving only a quivering sea-scape of light and shade under a mask of blurred grey. I turned and went automatically to the chest indicated by the witch-like Mistress Susannah. There were starchy drawers, a grey flannel petticoat, corsets, and an unbecoming high-necked dark dress – a cast-off probably, I thought distastefully – of my formidable visitor.

Of my other clothes there was no sign. A glimpse of them perhaps might have broken the spell I was under. As things were, the more I tried clarification, the more bewildered I became.

I took the garments out one by one, then went to the washstand and poured water from the ewer into the basin. It was icy cold, and the soap smelled strongly of carbolic. After I'd washed I dressed, and glanced at myself through the shabby mirror that had a crack in one corner.

I looked awful.

Pale hair hanging loose on either side of a thin colourless face that had dark rings under the eyes. Was that *me*? Did I always look like that? A rush of sudden vanity temporarily dispelled fear and other emotions. I picked up a comb and a few hairpins from the dressing table, and drew the hair, which was quite thick, to the back of my head in a knot. The drab gown of course only emphasized my bad points. A touch of mascara could have drawn attention to my eyes which were really quite good – a kind of soft violet with thick dark lashes under fly-away brows. I stared round for a reticule and had a start.

My head jerked.

Mascara? – a reticule? – what made me think of such things? Did they hold some clue to my past, were they the first step to remembering? I stood quite still for a moment waiting for an answer. It didn't come. The words must have been just a meaningless imprint left on my mind.

I was rubbing my cheeks to bring colour to them when the key turned in the door and my gaoler marched in again carrying a tray. She put it down on a small pedestal table near the window and said brusquely, 'There's a bowl of good wholesome porridge that should put some life into you, and a slice of bread spread with fish paste. No time to make toast when the master takes service.' She paused, and added sharply, 'Well, show a bit of gratitude, girl. A thank you wouldn't be out of place, and draw that stool up.' She waved an arm towards a high three-legged piece of rough deal furniture. 'I'm not waiting on you more than's necessary. Quick now.'

The hot blood rushed to my face. 'My ankle's very painful,' I said, 'and you have no right to speak to me like that—'

'Right? *Right?*' she echoed explosively. 'And who are *you* to defy me?'

'That's just it,' I interrupted. 'Who? *You* tell me I'm the wife of someone called Llarne. If so, and I've had an accident as you say, I think *I* myself have every right to see him and ask him to explain.'

I expected another angry exclamation, but to my surprise she quietened down and answered in more conciliatory tones. 'Now, now. There's no need to be huffed. It's your well-being I'm thinking of. After the shock of the fall you need looking after, and that means being brought back to act as normal as possible. Running this big house is a full-time job for me, and if my tongue has a sharp edge to it sometimes you must try and understand. So just you get on with your breakfast now, and it won't be long before you greet your husband.'

Obviously, whoever Mr Justin Llarne might be, whether my husband or not, he had influence with her, and wouldn't want complaints from me of her behaviour.

I said nothing, and she turned with another characteristic jerk of her head and left the room, locking the door, as before, behind her.

The porridge was milky and sweet, and although it didn't tempt me I swallowed it, but left the bread with its odious fishy smell. I suppose I must have needed food, because afterwards I felt considerably better, and decided that when I came face to face with my alleged spouse, I would do my best to show no fear, but act with as much dignity as possible.

The meeting occurred earlier than I'd expected. About an hour had passed when Mistress Susannah came back looking smartened up wearing a starched apron over her long black skirt, and her ginger hair pushed tidily back under a small white bonnet.

She glanced at me critically and said with unexpected approval, 'That's better. You look more fit now to meet respectable gentlemen. Master Silas is back from chapel now an' you're to see him in the study before Mr Justin arrives.'

My heart quickened as I followed her from the room – not only through apprehension, but with a throb of excitement. Now, surely I should learn more about the strange circumstances leading to the sorry state I was in. A corridor led to the right from the door. I followed her austere figure past a flight of stairs and two other doors which were both closed, taking from there a sharp cut that ended abruptly in what was, presumably, the study. A chink of eerie light filtered along the landing from a narrow stained-glass window high up on the wall near to the door. My wardress – I could no longer think of her as anything else – turned and beckoned with a bony finger. 'See you're polite to the master,' she said, 'he's likely to be tired after ministering to his flock.'

She ushered me inside. It was a drab room – everything appeared brown or grey, containing a desk, high-backed chairs, and one wall completely filled with books. The heavy table had what looked like a large Bible on it, although a faint mingled smell of spirits and tobacco permeated the air. A beam of light from the single window fell slantwise across a stiff-backed male figure seated directly opposite the door. His pale face was long and sad-looking – rather like a tired sheep, I thought irrelevantly with a touch of unexpected humour. But when he got to his feet and came towards me any faint lifting of my brief lighter mood changed. There was nothing tired about Master Silas. His eyes, though small, were shrewd and dark and piercing. His long line of a mouth, very like his sister's, had a ruthless determination that brought all my apprehension flooding back.

He smiled, and the gesture did nothing to help. It was somehow intimidating, holding a warning and a threat beneath the façade of welcome. Or perhaps being so tensed up I imagined this; I don't know.

He was tremendously tall, slightly stooping, reminding me of some gigantic black bird of prey in his black-tailed coat. An arm shot out to take my hand.

'Ah! Mistress Llarne!' he said, gripping my palm. 'You're feeling better, I hope. A pity you should have had such an unfortunate experience. You must do all you can to get better now, must you not? And we in our turn will take care of your welfare. This is the wish of my good friend, your husband, who will arrive shortly.'

I didn't like his looks, his touch or his voice that carried a thin sound through the teeth resembling a hiss. There was nothing about him to restore confidence. I was suddenly once more terribly afraid.

'There's no need to be nervous,' he said. 'You are suffering from shock, my dee-ar.' The 'dear' was drawn out, ingratiatingly. 'Mr Justin will soon be able to put you at ease, I am sure. So trust in the Almighty and your friends, and all will be well.'

Another bland smile crossed the long face.

Momentary giddiness swam over me. Memories struggled at the back of my mind, searching through confusion for recognition. Nothing of sense registered. For a few seconds I almost fell, and only through a tensed effort of will managed to retain balance.

The mist before my eyes cleared bringing the unpleasant countenance into focus again.

'Perhaps I shall remember him when I see him,' I managed to say lamely.

'Perhaps – perhaps,' he echoed. 'Let us hope so.' But the 'hope' held no conviction.

I felt suffocated in a nightmare web of lies and intrigue which was only diverted temporarily by the reopening of the door. Master Silas and his sister moved aside and stood in the shadows watching as a man entered. It was like a scene in a play. He was tallish, broad, with curling black hair and side-burns. At a quick glance contact between us was electric as though an unseen wire was sprung to hold us – I was aware of his bold stance, a certain swagger and contempt that stimulated me beyond present circumstances or the future.

A challenge.

'So!' he said, and his voice, though hard, was cultured. 'Here you are, after your fool's trick!'

I had the nerve to answer boldly, 'Here I am, and I hope you'll be able to tell me exactly *who*, and—'

'Sit *down*,' he said imperiously, indicating a short bench.

I did so, but my eyes never left his own. They were cold, bright piercing grey under dark brows, as brilliant, when the light caught them, as the shining buttons on his brown velvet jacket. Had he dressed for my attention? It rather appeared so, and the possibility gave me courage to add, 'Will you explain now, please?'

'Impertinent as ever are you, madam? Well—' He lifted a forefinger warningly. 'You're getting no more explanations than you've already had. As my wife you'll see you give these good people no further trouble and do what you can to aid Mistress Susannah if she wants anything done about the house. That will satisfy me. I shan't bother you in any way. You can be assured of your privacy.' He paused, then continued, 'On the other hand, if I have any legitimate complaint of your behaviour from Master or Mistress Trevanion, you will answer to me and be sorry. I have knowledge of how to deal with a rebellious woman or girl.'

He went to the door, turned, and looking at me once more before leaving, remarked in slightly more conciliatory tones, 'Eat well, and what you're given. I noticed you limped slightly when you went to the chair. No doubt Mistress Susannah will find liniment for your ankle. And don't be in any hurry to return to my home. Under the circumstances, I prefer my own company.'

The door closed.

He was gone.

I was left with Master Silas and his sister, and I was trembling, but not only from fear this time.

Presently, Mistress Susannah accompanied me back to the tawdry bedroom, leaving me alone under lock and key, with the wind rising again outside and the thunderous breaking of the waves against the rocks below.

2

During the next few days I began to feel better physically, although I was strictly confined to the drab bedroom. Mistress Susannah bound and attended to my ankle, and brought some concoction of her own for the bruise on my head and any minor cuts. The food was served up in a more appetizing manner – on the instructions of Master Silas, I supposed, or Justin Llarne, and I was given a travel book to read. One morning linen was brought that needed mending, and a box of needles and thread.

'No use brooding,' I was told brusquely. 'Useful activity's a help for curing brain troubles. And there's plenty waiting for a spare pair of hands.'

'If I knew *what* was the matter with my brain,' I couldn't help saying, 'it would be a help too. You haven't told me much. Only that I had a fall. Have I seen a doctor?'

'*Doctor*? Why would we pay one of them money-grabbers when there's the master on the spot. Better qualified Master Silas is than any of those high-falutin' swaggering creatures.'

Her scorn deflated me.

'Oh. I didn't know. Is Master Silas an apothecary then or something?'

'Apothecary? Now don't go using such long fancy words to me, girl. Curiosity killed the cat – haven't you heard of that?'

The words had a familiar ring, though I didn't know from where. I just shrugged and looked away. She gave me a huff and click of the tongue, turned and left. This time she didn't lock the door, but I knew if I attempted to leave she would be watching.

Gales had risen and blown up during the day and once more swirling veils of thin sand blew against the window shrouding sea and sky into uniformity.

Pressing my face against the glass I could just perceive two blurred small shapes swaying and rocking like ghost ships against the dimmer horizon of sea and sky. Why would they be out in such uncertain weather, I wondered. Fishing?

As I watched they disappeared behind a lump of granite coastland stretching its monstrous rocky tongue into the water. The clouds of foam and sand thickened with renewed force driving an icy draught of wind through the window cracks; I was about to pull the curtains close when a rumble of low laughter jerked me to rigid attention.

I may have been immobile for only two seconds, but when I turned I had a further shock. Something or some*one* was standing near and staring at me from small eyes in a broad egg-shaped face. He had a large head surmounted by a red cap pulled down behind large ears. His short legs were covered by patched trousers and a jersey reached from his shoulders almost to the knees.

Obviously a half-wit.

' 'Ullo,' he said in a hoarse, croaking voice with spittle leaking down one side of his chin. 'Good night edn't et? Wot's you looken' fur? Eh?' The grin faded suddenly; he frowned and poked his head forward like a bull about to charge.

I drew back quickly and at that moment the door opened and Mistress Susannah swept in. She caught hold of the poor creature by one ear and as he cringed cuffed him on a cheek smartly.

'You've no business here. You'll get my stick to your back if I ever catch you upstairs again,' she cried roughly. 'Come along now, back where you belong.'

She marched him away, turned before leaving, and told me, 'This is Jed. He collects wood and does odd jobs and scrubbing when I want. He won't harm you. But keep your door shut proper if I forget to lock it. Saves any temptation, just in case. See?'

I didn't of course. Only one thing registered in my mind – that other things as well as an unknown and unrecognizable husband haunted the world of my lost memory, and that I was no nearer solving the mystery than I had been when I woke up in this strange place.

For a week nothing spectacular happened. My foot and ankle steadily improved, and Mistress Susannah became slightly more conciliatory – probably on Master Silas's instructions – allowing me to take the restricted short walk along the dingy landings in which the dusty smell of spirits and tobacco tinged with something else – something more personal like that of old clothes – still lingered. I longed for fresh air, but the small narrow windows I passed were either of stained glass, high up in the wall, or tightly closed and barred. When I mentioned the study Miss Susannah bridled instantly.

'That room ed'n for you,' she said flatly. 'It's the master's private place. No woman's allowed there except on rare occasions; very rare – like that meeting you had with Mr Justin – so bear that in mind and remember.'

I could hardly forget. Except on isolated occasions I knew the key to the study door was generally turned in the lock following cleaning sessions. However, one day after its generally assiduous caretaker's departure downstairs, I ventured further than usual along the maze of corridors and noticed that a chink of light streamed from the forbidden room.

Making as certain as possible that no unpleasant visitant like the trespassing half-wit was lurking by any shadowed corner, I went cautiously ahead though as quickly as my ankle permitted, and entered Master Silas's sanctum. It was mid-morning, and I had to blink my eyes against the rush of silvered sunlight which gave sudden sharp clarity to the faded carpet, old-fashioned furniture and lined walls of books. A map lay on the table, and the desk was open with a few papers outspread there. There was also a large tele-scope standing on a plinth directly facing the open door.

A man's room.

I crossed to the window. The view showed a clear expanse of the narrow bay bordered on each side by rugged coast. The tide was low, and the sea calm beyond the pale sands. All was a panorama of light and shade reflecting the ice-cut sharpness of a fine line-etching on glass. I noticed to my right something that had not been visible from the window of my bedroom – what appeared to be the tall chimney-stack of a building jutting up from the far side of the cliff. I was wondering about this and whether it was tenanted, if so by whom, when the grating of the door and tread of footsteps startled me.

I jerked round and to my astonishment saw Justin Llarne standing there. My heart hammered against my ribs. I don't recall what he was wearing – all that registered in those few seconds of confrontation was the fierce unswerving gleam of his eyes on my face. His stare told me nothing, either hostile or friendly. But a challenge was there, and I forced myself to face it, lifting my head an inch higher.

'You're not supposed to be here,' he said.

'So Mistress Susannah told me,' I replied. 'But I got bored, and the door was open. I've not harmed anything.'

'Perhaps not. All the same, as my wife—' I could feel the hot blood mounting my face. 'As my wife—' he reiterated, 'you're supposed to be in her charge temporarily, and for your own sake it would be best not to defy her – or me.'

I tore my gaze from his. 'Very well, I'll go.'

I swept past, but before my hand reached the door he'd swung me round and the hot pressure of his lips was on my own. Then, still holding my arm, he said, 'That is for now, Mrs Llarne. Don't annoy me further. I shan't trouble you any more so long as you keep your place and stay out of my sight. I've no use for a ridiculous spoiled young woman. Go now. Away with you, before I put you over my knee.'

Humiliated, hardly able to breathe for indignation, I cried, 'You've no business to act like that. You—'

'No.' Suddenly he laughed. 'Don't tempt me. Now – off with you before I keep my word.'

I fled.

The memory of his laughter was still in my ears when I reached the bedroom. Yet depression had vanished in a whirl of angry excitement. There was something magnetic about him despite his ill manners.

He'd called himself my husband. But he *couldn't* be. Surely I would never have married such a bullying creature.

Or would I?

Once more the strange circumstances of my predicament overwhelmed me, and I wondered if I should wake up presently from some strange bizarre dream to ordinary life. But what *was* ordinary life, and where?

Fear began slowly to cloud my brain again, and for once I wasn't sorry when Mistress Susannah brought me my mid-morning drink. It was one of her own concoctions – fruity and sweetish, with an agreeable tang and flavour to it.

'Have you got a fever again?' she asked, eyeing me shrewdly as I took the first sip. 'There's a high colour on your cheeks.'

'I don't *feel* hot,' I told her, and at that moment it was true. Little icy rivulets of moisture were gathering at the back of my head and coursing down my spine.

'Hm. Well – have a lie down for a bit. The sooner you're in proper health again the better it will be for all of us – especially Mr Justin.'

I shivered.

'Am I that important to him?' I couldn't resist saying rashly. 'I wouldn't have thought so.'

She frowned. 'What do you mean? Can it be that you're remembering something?' Despite the sharp voice I detected a hint of underlying anxiety in its tone.

I shook my head.

'No. I only wish it was true. But I shall one day, I *know* it. Concussion doesn't last forever, and when I do – when I get the first tiny clue—'

'Yes?' The word came out like a pistol shot.

I sighed. 'Oh, I don't know. It all depends.'

'Playing games are you? Trying to confuse us all? You should be ashamed, you should really. After what we're trying to do for you. Here am I, ready to wait on you hand and foot, cook you tasty meals, and trudge up and down stairs attending to your comfort with not even a thank you or sign of gratitude in return.' She broke off with her mouth turned into a button of disapproval.

'I'm sorry, Mistress Susannah,' I lied meekly.

Her small black eyes narrowed. Clearly she didn't believe me, and after a toss of her head, she turned and marched out in her characteristic mannish way.

I finished the drink, and a feeling of lassitude, which was almost pleasant, crept over me. My thoughts relaxed from the constant strain of trying to recall my past life to conjectures of the present and the future. *If* by any fantastic fact it could be proved to me I was really the wife of the detestable but colourful character called Justin Llarne, where had been our home together until my accident? Or didn't we have one? And the telescope in the study – to whom did it belong? Master Silas probably, since that particular room was his sanctum. Then what had been Justin's business there? Spying on me? But why? He'd certainly shown no concern for me; rather the reverse. It had been as though he'd enjoyed catching me out like a naughty child disobeying orders – which of course I had been. Suddenly I knew with a deepening sense of excitement that I should continue to take every chance that arose of solving the true problem of my identity, even though it might hold a spice of danger.

And that's how it was. But I was careful – very careful only to trespass on any forbidden territory when I was certain Master Silas and Justin Llarne were both off the premises. This was not difficult. During those first few weeks I discovered the days on which the master of the house left for chapel, or for the village which was a mile or so inland out of sight of the house. This was habitual on a Monday; Mistress Susannah had let out to me in one of her rare pleasanter, more conversational moods, that he regularly visited the post office in Cragley on that morning for financial reasons – which I presumed meant drawing out or cashing an order to pay weekly household expenses, and for any extra shopping she needed doing. On these occasions, Justin Llarne could generally be seen out in his boat fishing, and Mistress Susannah was occupied for certain hours in household affairs.

So I felt more free at such times to do a little careful investigating.

By then it was autumn. Even if Mistress Susannah had not referred to 'the wild autumn tides' one day, I would have known by the yellowing of the late leaves on a windblown scraggy sycamore tree outside. At times, thick mists rolled in from the sea obscuring the tumped moorland hills inland, and curdling the rim of sullen sky and water into obscurity. My gaoler – I could still think of her as nothing else – insisted on treating me as a semi-invalid, although my foot and minor injuries had healed, serving her nourishing pick-me-up drinks which she made me take before meals. I suppose they *did* cheer me up. But as fears receded I grew intensely bored. Only the anticipation, tinged with apprehensive excitement, of coming face to face again with my supposed husband, gave any interest to my life. The memory of his rough embrace and one brief kiss still lingered in my thoughts whenever I allowed myself to recall the incident. His hot words and laughter rekindled indignation and a determination that when we *did* meet again, I would act differently, whatever the outcome, and not behave as the nervous, half-hysterical girl I must have appeared.

Although I continued to do any useful task that Mistress Susannah required, my growing restlessness must have shown, because she said one afternoon, 'Master Silas has suggested you have a meal downstairs with us tonight. As you have behaved reasonably lately I have agreed. Mr Justin'll be here, so you'll have a chance for a chat together. Only short, of course, he'll be off to his home afterwards. Estate matters to attend to.'

Despite my resentment and dislike of Justin Llarne at our first two encounters, I couldn't help feeling a strange leap of my heart at the thought of facing him in what should be pleasanter circumstances. The idea of a fresh gown was also stimulating, even though I doubted that Mistress Susannah's taste would be mine. I couldn't imagine her having any fashion sense. But then, what *was* the fashion these days? I just didn't know, because whenever I made any effort to conjure up a past my mind still remained a blank. This fact was what was so terrifying, and at such moments I had somehow to force it away in case I went either truly mad, or screamed, beating my hands against the wall. Such occasions were rare. Thankfully the hope of recovery from the malady I was suffering from, whether it was concussion or sickness – quickly came to my rescue. Life was tolerable, that was all, helped I suppose by my daily small tasks given to me by Mistress Susannah, and by conjecture concerning the mysteries of the strange household.

When, an hour or two before the meal, Mistress Susannah laid the promised gown upon the bed, I was pleasantly surprised, in spite of the strong mothball smell emanating from its folds. Why, and how did I recall 'mothball' in those few moments? Just for a brief interim familiarity – a recognition of another life in another place somewhere in the past titillated my senses. From the deep darkness memory stirred, then as quickly died, banished by the rough jarring of Mistress Susannah's voice.

'What's the matter with you, girl? Struck dumb are you? Be a little polite for once. That's a fine gown, fit for a real lady. You should be grateful for such a handsome dress to please your good man in, and I've taken the trouble, let me tell you, to stitch the neck higher, with a bit of extra lace at the front.'

I stared, then smiled and said, 'Thank you very much. Yes, it's – it's pretty.'

'Pretty? Tut-tut. Who wants *prettiness*? It has style and is in good taste. Mr Justin should approve *providing*' – she paused warningly, before adding – 'providing you play no tricks of sly alteration. If that happens there'll be trouble.'

I shook my head, promised her that I'd wear it just as it was, and apparently satisfied, she left.

When the sounds of her footsteps had faded I picked up the gown and held it in front of me before the shabby mirror. Only a limited view was visible, and the reflection was not very clear. But it was sufficient to please me, showing the dress to be of soft blue material cut simply with a row of tiny pearl buttons reaching down the bodice from the modest lace collar to just above the hips. The sleeves were bunched, drawn into tight lace cuffs, the skirt full, giving no slight indication of any feminine curves beneath. A modest picture indeed; but the gentle tones seemed to enhance rather than diminish what feminine qualities in looks I might possess, and when I arranged my hair from a centre parting to fall looped over the ears to a knot at the back, I was reminded of an illustration in one of the magazines Mistress Susannah had surprisingly lent me of a character in a story by Currer Bell.

For the first time since the strange events had brought me to this dark and lonely house I was jerked from depression on a wave of pleasurable curiosity. Whoever and whatever I was – whether wife or not, I was determined to appear the very best that present circumstances provided for the meal that evening.

I brushed my hair until it shone, before pinning it up, and shortly before Mistress Susannah arrived to take me downstairs, rubbed my pale cheeks vigorously to induce a little colour. Excitement added an extra glow, and when I faced her as she entered the bedroom I sensed she had a mild shock, whether of approval or envy, I couldn't say. But the thought occurred to me that she might not *genuinely* wish me to please her precious Mr Justin Llarne.

I almost giggled to myself; though when she led me downstairs just a tiny lurch of apprehension quickened my heart.

The main staircase must have been handsome once. It was wide, and the steps were of marble though chipped in places, having carved bannisters that ended on the ground floor with a dusty legendary figure holding a lamp. The carpeting was worn and thin. The strange indefinable odour of dust, mingled with something smelling vaguely like tobacco, thickened the air. A large cracked portrait of a woman with piled-up hair and a poodle dog on her lap stared from a heavy frame on the wall.

It was only later that I realized the oddness in my being able to recognize a poodle dog when I couldn't even remember my own real name.

I shall never forget – and I suppose that seems an odd thing to say, when I had forgotten so much – the moment of being ushered by Mistress Susannah into the dark old-fashioned room on the ground floor.

The interior, lit only by a filter of dying light streaking between heavy brown window curtains at the far end, and the flicker of candles in wall brackets, had its familiar musty smell about it, blended with that of cooking. Onions I guessed, or some kind of broth. A large mahogany sideboard loomed just inside at right angles to the door, and Silas was already seated in a high-backed carved chair at the end of a long refectory table, presiding as master of the house over his flock. Justin Llarne was ensconced on his right side, and Mistress Susannah directed me to a place facing him. She picked up a small handbell, rang it sharply, then took the chair obviously already reserved for her at the end of the table facing her brother.

'Good evening, my dear,' I heard Silas say in his usual mincing manner. 'How nice to have you with us and for you to meet your husband again. You are feeling better, I hope?'

'Yes, thank you,' I replied mechanically. Mistress Susannah's head gave a little nod of approval; across the table I was aware of Justin Llarne's eyes upon me inscrutably. He was wearing a bottle-green velvet jacket over a lemon waistcoat, with a white neckscarf and bow. There was something disconcerting about his motionless poise until he remarked suddenly, 'You have a fine colour tonight. I trust it's natural and not due to the rouge pot. I can assure you there's no need for artifice.'

Quickly angry, I bit my lip and retorted, 'I have no paint or powder and if I had I would not use any.'

'Good.'

I could sense Mistress Susannah bristling. She opened her mouth to speak, but at the same moment the door opened, and the girl employed occasionally to help with the housework appeared with a tureen of soup, followed

by Jed with a trolley bearing bowls and condiments and
cutlery.

Napkins were placed beside each bowl on the table.
Silas, looking like a gaunt, carved effigy in stone presiding
at some ancient ceremony, tucked his napkin into his
neckscarf, followed by Mistress Susannah and Justin. I did
the same, and there was a short pause before the master of
the house lifted a hand, bowed his head and uttered grace
in his thin voice.

There was a low chorus of 'amen' from the table, the
servant girl and Jed. Then a sudden stirring and tinkle of
pots and cutlery, and a rattle as the couple left, wheeling
the trolley back through the door.

Mistress Susannah lifted the large ladle and commenced
pouring the servings. An air of self-righteousness filled
the atmosphere. During the procedure of the dishes being
handed round, I had time to study Justin's expression. His
gaze was inscrutable, yet intent upon my own. I fancied a
twitch of humour lurked about his well-carved lips, but
his whole attitude was somehow compelling. It was as
though he was asserting, 'You may be in the Trevanions'
charge, but the power is mine. You are my wife.'

My senses stirred with a thrill of danger, of magnetism
that I couldn't dispel. His *wife*. Was I? *Was I*?

Feeling the warm blood come through my whole body
in a tide of crimson under the flimsy dress to my cheeks, I
tore my attention from his and took a first sip of broth.

It was savoury, quite appetizing, tasting of something
that was familiar but that for the moment I couldn't quite
place. Following the soup, game pie was served, and lardy
cake as a sweet. As the meal was apparently a special

occasion Master Silas had allowed a bottle of Mistress Susannah's home-brewed wine to be opened. It was extremely strong, and despite Silas's verbal condemnation of alcohol in general, he had two liberal portions of it. I wasn't really surprised. The whole house seemed to hold the faint smell of liquor blended with the pungent odour of tobacco, dust, and cooking. I had a shrewd idea Silas was an imbiber in secret, if not openly.

Looking back my memories of that strange period are hazy, holding the quality of a dream wherein events and places became distorted like the imaginings of a fairy-tale. Mistress Susannah assumed more and more the characteristics of a wily old witch plotting for her scheming brother's ends, and Justin – my conjecturing came to a halt when I considered the spectacular presence of the enigmatic and colourful personality of the man purporting to be my husband.

He said little during the meal but nobody appeared to have anything to discuss. Silas, I noticed, seemed unduly preoccupied with his food, and despite his previous air of importance and show of being master of the house, displayed a crude lapse of manners, gulping his drink, and at intervals smacking his lips volubly, drawing a hand across his mouth instead of using his napkin.

I was mildly disgusted, but not surprised; nothing about my odd situation surprised me any more – not even when Justin said to me at the end of the feast – for indeed it had been a feast – 'The time's come, methinks, for you and I to have a talk. I'm sure Mistress Susannah will agree?' And he gave a quick intimidating glance towards the stiff figure who was about to ring the bell for Jed.

'That's right. Just as you say Mr Justin,' Mistress Susannah remarked. Her brief glance at me was stern, almost fierce, as though to impress on me the necessity for obedience. 'Upstairs will you be going? To her room? Or—?'

He smiled ironically. 'Possibly. We'll have our chat first to save any titillating diversion. You can trust me to see she's properly taken care of.'

I could sense the woman bridling. 'Very well. If you have any further instructions for me concerning your – lady's – wellbeing I shall be near at hand.'

'Oh, I'm sure Mr Justin's aware of your admirable capacity for vigilance at all times, my dee-ah,' Master Silas commented in his thin squeaky tones.

Justin broke the unpleasant tension by gripping my arm and ushering me out into the main corridor where the girl and Jed were already wheeling the trolley, presumably down to the kitchen. After a few yards we took a short cut along a narrow side passage and through a door leading into a dingy conservatory. There was no sight or sound of the sea there. The atmosphere had an ancient sad air about it; the few plants appeared dejected and dusty, and tendrils from a vine hung from the glass roof, obviously needing water.

There was an iron seat immediately against the near wall, and at the far end of the room a parrot swung and screeched by its cage.

'Well now,' Justin said, 'don't just stand there.' He waved to a seat. 'Try and look comfortable even if you're not. Or are you afraid of getting dirt on that frilly thing?' He took a handkerchief from a pocket and gave a flip or two to the rusty iron.

I sat down abruptly. 'I'm not afraid of dust. This isn't *my* dress anyway. Mistress Susannah brought it for me just for tonight.'

'No doubt to charm me.'

'I've no idea what her intentions were,' I said sharply. 'And in any case since you've been *inflicted* upon me I've no need to charm, have I?'

His eyebrows shot up. I fancied there was a twitch of amusement at his lips, but a gleam of temper lit his eyes, and his voice was sharp when he retorted, 'Be careful you don't go too far. Let me remind you I'm not a man to take insolence from any woman – not even a wife.'

'But then how do I *know* I'm your wife?' I asked rashly.

'Are you asking me to prove it?'

'No. Yes – yes,' I told him recklessly. 'If you can, without – without—'

'Without violating any shred of virginity you may possess.' He gave a short laugh, then suddenly his mood changed. 'Don't worry. I've no fancy for a reluctant spouse. I've had chances enough already to trespass on your delightful privacy without asking permission had I wished.'

I flushed. Because of course this was true, although resentment mingled with relief filled me, that he had apparently so easily forgotten the impulsive embrace in the study.

I bit my lips and with an effort curbed any impatient retort. There was a second or two's pause, then he turned quickly, and with his hands behind his back walked a few paces away, allowing the parrot to fly squawking on to his shoulder. He stood staring through the dusty window, while I waited tensely for further reaction. He had a fine figure, very broad at the shoulders, but slim-hipped, with an arrogant poise. Once again, in spite of my dislike, I couldn't help the warm glow of excitement stirring my blood. It occurred to me that he and Silas must come from very different worlds. In the well-cut tailed velvet jacket and twill breeches, he had a certain distinction that set him apart from the rest of the household. Who *was* he then, in reality? And once more the old question – who was *I*?

He jerked round suddenly and shooed the parrot away, then strode decisively towards me, thrust out an arm, and pulled me to my feet again. His gaze was intent and compelling on my face.

'It's high time to have things straight between us,' he said coldly. 'And I warn you that unless you tell me everything you know and remember, you'll regret it. This is no game. Do you understand?'

I shook my head helplessly. 'No. I've been asked that so many times,' I answered.

Both his hands gripped my shoulders then slid to the softer flesh of my arms with more gentle pressure, 'Is that true? *Nothing*? Think back, think carefully – not one *small* fact about your past? With me? – Or otherwise?'

I closed my eyes briefly and shook my head. 'No – no. Nothing. The gargoyles at the gate before I fell, that's all.'

'If you're lying to me—'

'I'm not lying,' I broke in impatiently. 'Why should I?'

'Why indeed!' he said, with a curl of the lip that was not pleasant. 'God knows what any devious trick a woman gets up to if it's to her benefit.' There was a short pause before he added, 'And *you're* all woman whether you admit it or not. So have done with your innocent little-girl airs.'

His face was very near to mine. The strength of his personality threatened to overcome me. I pulled away sharply.

He laughed, and waved an arm in dismissal.

'Oh, for the *Lord*'s sake spare the prudery. Though you may believe it or not my intentions are strictly honourable – if a man may be said in such a matter to be honourable to his wife.'

'But—'

'And don't interrupt. I *should* say – I wish to help.'

'*Help*? How can you? When—'

'When so far I may have appeared somewhat – heavy-handed?' he interrupted. His tone was wary. 'My dear girl there are times a man has to assert his position. Now then' – he broke off, eyeing me closely before continuing, 'again – I'm asking you – have you a *shadow* even, of memory, following your fall?'

'No,' I answered wearily. 'I've told you and *told* you, told everyone – Mistress Susannah and Master Silas – *I don't remember anything.*'

'Hm.' At last he seemed to believe me and said more quietly, 'Very well. But *if* and *when* you do, I want you to come straight to me, or get Mistress Susannah to tell me and I'll be with you as soon as possible. Understand? Not a word to anyone else.'

I nodded.

'By the way, have you any complaints about your treatment here? Or the food? Do you eat well?'

'I didn't at first,' I told him, 'but now I do. In fact the meals have become quite tasty. Especially the savouries, and broth. I suppose I should thank Mistress Susannah for that. At the beginning whenever I refused to eat she seemed quite concerned. So,' I shrugged, 'well, there seemed no point in arguing and getting too weak, so I gave in.'

'Hm! And what about sleep? Do you get good nights?'

'She sees to that too. I have a potion.'

'Is it necessary, do you think?'

Surprised that my opinion should be asked on anything concerning household routine, I answered, 'I've no idea. I suppose it *is* pleasanter not to lie awake problemizing and questioning and wondering all night, but the air's stuffy. Yes – that *could* be better. I so long to be not a prisoner, and be able to go outside for a bit.'

'I'll see if that can be arranged,' he said unexpectedly.

'With Mistress Susannah?'

'Yes, with Mistress Susannah.' His voice was curt once more, his manner remote and factual.

'Thank you.'

After that, little more was said between us. He went to the door, opened it and waited for me to leave, making no gesture of familiarity or showing further interest. I was mildly piqued, recalling once more that first passionate kiss in the study. Then just as quickly resentment returned. Resentment that this overbearing stranger – for to me he was still a stranger, who purported to be my husband – should have such power over me. So I lifted my head with a haughty gesture, held my skirt with one hand a few inches above one toe, and swept past. The familiar, tall gaunt shape, who obviously had been lurking about in the corridor eager to catch a possible word between us, emerged from the shadows.

'Here is your charge, Mistress Susannah,' I heard Justin say to her hatefully, followed by, 'Behave yourself, wife dear, remember my instructions,' and then to my gaoler again, 'I have a few points to discuss with you later, Mistress Trevanion, ma'am. For the moment, you may as well continue as usual.'

Seething with indignation, I allowed myself to be shepherded upstairs again to my boring bedroom, wondering how much longer I would have to endure such frustration.

Next day I had a surprise.

After a breakfast of gruel and toast, Mistress Susannah arrived, carrying a brown cape thing over her arm. Her expression was grim and slightly flustered-looking. 'You're to go out,' she said, 'on Mr Justin's orders. Put this on. There's a bit of a wind. It wouldn't do for you to give any more complaints, would it?'

Trying to ignore her tone, exhilarated by the thought of getting fresh air at last, I put the cape round my shoulders saying, 'Thank you. I made no complaints. Only told my – told Mr Llarne – it would be nice to go out for a bit for air.'

'Hm!'

She shepherded me downstairs and along a maze of ill-lit corridors towards the kitchen quarters, eventually cutting off down a side passage that opened on to a granite flagged courtyard. The tangy, sweet-salty smell of brine and heather swept keenly into my nostrils as a number of gulls rose squawking into the air. I took a deep breath and lifted my face to the turbulent sky, shaking my hair from my face in the wind. From below the crash of waves thundered from the shore. My sudden wild sense of freedom must have quickened my pace. Mistress Susannah's hard grip was quickly on my arm pulling me back.

'There's no need to run,' she said sharply. 'You'll not be going down there. Just for a breath of air, Mr Justin said. No further than the gate – ever. You'll do well to remember it.'

I said nothing more at that point, but as we crossed the rising ground overlooking the shore I reminded her that as Mrs Llarne I was obviously expected to recall the locality sometime, and surely a glimpse of something and somewhere familiar in the past might help my memory.

'I'm not arguing with you,' came the short reply. 'Those are my instructions from your husband. To you, through *me*. And I'm abidin' with 'em.'

Through annoyance she'd lapsed into her earlier rough tones of speech, and I wondered, not for the first time, what her previous status had been in Master Silas's household. Was she *really* his sister? Probably; neither of them somehow seemed to fit satisfactorily into their present situation. And what was the truth of Justin's relationship with them?

I was vaguely pondering the question when a wild gust of wind caught my headscarf, took it up into the air and blew it some yards ahead. I rushed after it, followed the next second by Mistress Susannah who caught my shoulder in a vice like grip.

'Come back – come back. Let it be—' she screamed. 'It's steep over there—'

I stopped, watching the flimsy thing whirled away like some creature of the air itself, dipping and swirling into

wild clouds of blown foam. By then we were not far from
the gate in the wall marking the boundary of the mansion
territory. The view beyond showed a stretch of steep cliff
sloping sharply to the breaking sea. To the right there
loomed the silhouetted shape of the building I'd seen from
the window with its tall chimney jutting starkly above the
jagged finger of rock. Just for an instant a beam of light
caught a long monastic-looking window. I brushed my hair
from my damp forehead to get a clearer view, but Mistress
Susannah wrenched me round, dragging me ruthlessly
away in a grip hard and strong as a man's.

'Keep y're eyes off Falk,' she shrilled. 'That place is not
for you till you've sense enough in y'r head to recognize it.'

'What do you mean?' I cried. '*Recognize?*'

She didn't answer until we reached a more sheltered spot
well behind the courtyard walls. Then, when we'd both
sufficient breath to speak reasonably, she said crossly, 'You
want an answer to everything, don't you? But because of
your being Mr Justin's wife, and out of respect for him, I'll
try and keep my temper, though sake's alive! – it's not easy,
with such a defiant miss as you, and if you'd been my
daughter you'd have felt the slap of my hand before now.
Still, that place you had your eye on is *his* – and could have
been yours now, along with him, if you hadn't got yourself
into such a mess. A handsome mansion it is – one of the
finest in all Cornwall. And I hope one day you'll have
earned the right to be there. But for the present just try and
be grateful for what you have, a good bed and food, and
thank the good Lord and Master Silas you're not lying at the
bottom of the cliffs waiting f'r the gulls to pecky y'r flesh.'

Following this outburst she stuck her jaw out, quickened

our steps again and with an air of triumph brought me to the door of the house.

I shivered at the macabre picture she'd painted of me lying a mangled corpse on that cold grim beach, and for the first time I wondered if she was trying deliberately to frighten me to death.

But if she was she wouldn't succeed, I told myself firmly. In a funny kind of way I was beginning to feel that compared to the sinister Silas Trevanion and his unprepossessing sister, Justin Llarne – whether my husband or not – had a sneaking sense of friendliness for me.

There was no more conversation between myself and Mistress Susannah before I reached my own room. As we passed the foot of the stairs I glimpsed the squat form of Jed standing hunched and watchful from a shadowed corner. He had a stubby finger in his mouth which fell to his side revealing a senile grin as we went by. Half-wit he might be, I thought distastefully, but a certain unpleasant primeval force seemed to emanate from the shapeless form that was threatening with a dark atavistic knowledge.

Mistress Susannah appeared not to notice him, and a minute later I was back in the gloomy bedroom alone, with the door locked, once more a prisoner.

There were sheets for me to mend, and other items to be darned laid out on the bed. Boring work, but better than having nothing to do; and so the day passed like the others in that awful household – how many there'd been I'd forgotten to count, but I knew it was not many.

The food was extra tasty that day, and I even got a

faint smile – more of a grimace really – from Mistress Susannah when I praised it.

Perhaps I had eaten too much, I don't know. But that night I had a bizarre dream.

I was struggling through a suffocating fog towards an immense towered shape with holed windows and a gaping door of a mouth that opened menacingly as I approached. Its power was magnetic. I had to press on, though my feet would hardly move, giving a terrifying sensation of being glued to the ground. There was no sound but a dismal wailing like that of some tortured spirit needing help. I tried to call but my voice wouldn't work, and when I reached the gap ahead, everything crumbled, and the massed shadow broke into a hideous crowd of swarming gargoyled shapes with hungry grinning jaws and lusting fingers reaching for my throat. I could hardly breathe; but before I fell, a wild scream of 'Jeremiah – Jeremiah' pierced my brain zigzagging in fiery lettering across the foggy air. *'Jeremiah—'*

I came to myself with the name still ringing in my ears; and looking up saw Mistress Susannah's long pale face staring down on me, above a swaying oil lamp.

'What's all this then?' she shrieked. 'Jeremiah! What's that to you? And what d'you mean waking the household up in th' middle of th' night? *Tell* me you little vixen.'

She pressed her macabre visage close to my face, and instinctively I shrank back into the pillow.

'A dream,' I said. 'A nightmare.'

There was a pause before she asked, 'What's that name mean to you – Jeremiah?'

I shook my head. 'Nothing. Absolutely nothing. I wish it did. It might help.'

'Who? – you? Or those of us here?' The question was short and sharp as a bullet from a gun.

I was surprised by her vehemence. Her narrowed eyes were blazing like those of some giant cat.

'Everyone's I should have thought. You're always pressing me about my memory. That's the reason I'm kept here, isn't it? – for me to get better and able to continue my life as it was?' I broke off, watching a confused flush mount her face.

'All right, all right. No need to argue. And no insolence, girl. It's plain to me your jaunt outside's been bad for you. I shall have to report this incident to Mr Justin. We can't have the whole household disturbed in such a way. I'm going to give you an extra draught now. So lie down quietly while I get it.'

Her discomfiture was so obvious it gave me courage.

'If I do,' I said, loudly and clearly, 'if you try and force anything on me, I shall report it to Mr Llarne. I don't want a draught or potion, and if you refuse to allow me out again I'll make trouble. I'm tired of being threatened and bullied. If Justin is really my husband he's a right to know what's going on. I've had an awful nightmare, but it's over now, and I'd like to rest. Do you mind?'

I faced her coldly, and she gasped.

'You – dare – to – talk – like – that – to – me!'

'Yes,' I told her, and I think I smiled faintly.

I felt strange, more in control, and had a feeling that whoever and whatever the name 'Jeremiah' signified to Mistress Susannah and her odious brother Silas, it marked a step forward through the fog of my amnesia.

She muttered something under her breath, turned, and

without another word left the room, closing the door with a slam.

Triumph filled me. I knew for the first time since my incarceration in that musty mansion a sense of direction for the future, and how to play my cards.

The day passed uneventfully, becoming misty at the end of the morning.

When evening came the weather cleared slightly giving fitful patches of thin moonlight through slowly rolling galleons of clouds. There was a sufficient slight wind to send occasional shadowed shapes across the pale sands – shapes which I recognized at intervals as real figures.

From the limited side angle of my window I caught the fitful glimmer of a light flashing above the humped tongue of rock stretching into the water beyond the Llarne house; its silouette now was indistinguishable, but for a second, when a thin sliver of light momentarily pierced the weird scene, the tall chimney was startlingly clear. Then all was dark again. I felt my muscles tense. Something was happening out there. Beyond the mournful monotonous thud of waves on the shore a muted murmur of activity thrummed the night silence. I kept my eyes riveted firmly ahead, and presently glimpsed a longish shape cutting to the beach where it slipped into the cliff's shadows and was lost. After that visibility became completely swathed again into a return of thickening mist. The vaporous air crept through the window cracks and under the bedroom door, dimming the mirror, lifting the thin matting and rug on the floor as though some insidious elemental entity threatened the whole area.

Shivering with sudden cold I left the window and

returned to the bed, pausing at the door for a few moments with my ears alert. There was a muffled tread of footsteps from below, followed by the sound of muted voices.

Then silence.

Despite the chill of my body, my senses were alert. Although my memories of the past were so limited, recalling only impersonal impressions of years gone by, I was aware, nevertheless, of certain historical events and had no doubts whatever that I'd been witnessing some kind of smuggling.

Then of what?

By whom? And where did I fit into the picture?

This I was determined to discover if I was allowed to live to do so.

3

For the next few weeks I was particularly careful to appear comparatively amenable to Mistress Susannah, and her vigilance relaxed slightly. She was sufficiently careless at odd moments to leave the bedroom door unlocked when she left after bringing the food, or leaving instructions concerning the boring tasks for me to perform. This was partly due to the fact that Master Silas developed a cold for which he demanded her considerable attention. I heard him moaning and groaning from below, and her fussing and soothing like a mother hen with a great scrawny chick. I could well imagine the scene and could feel only contempt, guessing he was not nearly so sick as he made out. The smell of spirits drifted up the stairs, and this brief diversion from her watchfulness gave me a chance for moments of exploration along the maze of landings. I found a side window that showed a clear view of my supposed earlier home of Falk, where Justin was now said to live alone. Although half hidden behind the rocks it was impressive, and in one moment of clarity from screwed-up eyes, I could perceive a thin track leading from below the gate of the courtyard of 'my prison' in a curving snake-like line down and round that jagged bleak peninsula towards the imposing granite structure.

My curiosity intensified. With a receding of previous fear, determination hardened in me somehow to discover for myself its size and perhaps obtain an idea of its locality – even some slight clue, however small, that might break the frustrating block in mind and memory.

The opportunity arrived earlier even than I'd hoped for. Mistress Susannah caught her brother's infection, which she naturally blamed on me for dragging her out and loitering in a sharp gale.

'As if I hadn't enough to do in running the household and looking after Master Silas without having to deal with the whims of a half-witted girl,' she grumbled before retiring to her room early one afternoon shortly after the event. 'Don't you get up to any mischief while I relaxes f'r 'n hour or so, and see that pillowslip's mended neat 'n proper. No cobblin' up in any old fashion or there'll be trouble.'

'I'll do it for you,' I told her, hating her manner, her bossiness, her looks, and everything about her with her long red nose and thin turned-down mouth, her sniffing and watchful screwed-up bleary eyes; she had a glass of whisky in her hand, and I had a sudden longing to grab it from her hand and smash it. But I managed to restrain the impulse. My aloof manner must have registered something of the contempt I felt. She stared at me for a moment speechless, as though trying to assess my mood, then she turned, gave a jerk of her head, which had a towel round it, and left with the usual slam of the door.

I waited for what I judged was about half an hour and tried the knob. Luckily the lock was undone; in her miserable state she'd forgotten to turn the key.

I went cautiously along the landing to the stairs. A black shawl was hanging conveniently from a peg nearby. I pulled it round me and waited for some seconds to be sure no Jed was lurking about. All was still and quiet except the distant intermittent rumble from the direction of the study of what sounded like gross snoring.

Master Silas probably, I thought, having one of his siestas after a suspicious late night and day's activity. If so I was comparatively safe from any unpleasant vigilance. The daily girl I knew had left. I'd heard her high voice screeching earlier, 'Going now', followed by some grunting avowal from Mistress Susannah. During my stay on the hateful premises my hearing had grown abnormally acute, I suppose the natural outcome of being alert to every small sound and echo of the present. When you can't remember, you key all your senses to visualizing what's going on, and to foreseeing the possible future.

I went downstairs safely through the cloying atmosphere of dust and cobwebs that seemed to drain the very air of life. The light also was misted, and dimmed by shadows; at the turn in the hall leading to the kitchen quarters I took the opposite direction from the passage leading to the back and courtyard where I'd gone with Mistress Susannah, and cut along the main wider corridor to what presumably ended at the front door.

I paused for a moment on reaching it, and found surprisingly that it was slightly ajar. My gentle push made only a slight creak, but startled, I waited motionless for a fraction of time hunched into the shadows until I was certain no one had heard.

Then, furtively, with my head huddled down into the shawl, I slipped out through a porch into a freshening wind.

It was a grey day. Lines of wan wind-blown trees waved their thin branches in the damp air on either side of a desolate drive that curved snake-like to a road above.

I looked up and round, and my heart quickened as recognition hit me with a shock.

They were the same – the immense grotesque gargoyle faces that formed my last contact with memory. The lane above too – leading at a crossroads on one side to the grouped moorland hills, and on the other showing a distant glimmer of glassy sea beyond a stretch of moor. I stepped forward to gain a better view of the latter and managed to locate the dark huddled silhouette of what must be a hamlet crouched against a hill ahead, and below that to the left, a building with a tall chimney appearing to be perched on the very edge of the cliffs stretching into the water.

Falk!

What did this mean? Had that remote deserted-looking mansion really once been my home with Justin Llarne? If so, what business had drawn me across the moor along the lonely road to this place of my imprisonment in too shocked a state to recall events before my fall?

No, no. It wouldn't do, I told myself stubbornly. I was

not his wife. If I'd ever lain with him in passion or known a close relationship my physical senses would have known.

Only one figment of memory jerked somewhere at the back of my brain in odd moments, and that didn't make sense. It was Jeremiah! – just a name; the name in my nightmare that had so infuriated Mistress Susannah.

I turned and went back into the dark hall. The hollow tread of footsteps at the far end alerted me to pause in the shadows. And the next minute I saw the gaunt tall form of Mistress Susannah passing from the back regions somewhere towards the kitchens. She looked like some giant dressed-up scarecrow in her drab clothes. I waited until all was silent again, then made my way apprehensively back to the bedroom wondering if she'd been investigating there.

She hadn't.

Everything was the same as when I'd left.

I didn't bother my brain any more at that point about wondering what my next move would be. I knew.

I would keep watch that night for any suspicious happenings at sea, and on the first opportunity make my way to Falk.

Justin held the key to my true identity.

Somehow, in some way I was determined to get his co-operation.

During the next few days – or rather nights, I became uneasily aware of mysterious, even sinister happenings at sea. Because of physical inactivity I was too restless to sleep soundly and spent much of the time listening to every small furtive movement or whisper from below, or peering through the window across the dark stretch of sea and sky. Intensity gave meaning which could have been true or not to the slightest sign of a boat's dimmed shape steering towards the coastline round Falk. Night fishing went on, of course, which could provide an innocent explanation. But I sensed, with curious certainty, that there was more to what went on than that. On two occasions diamond-bright pinpoints of light flashed from the claw-like headland, followed some time later by another from further out at sea. Once, in a shaft of pale moonlight, I had a momentary glimpse of a large brig silhouetted motionless and dark against a blurred sky. The next moment it was swamped by sullen cloud into furred oblivion.

Always, following such incidents, Mistress Susannah appeared more vigilant of my activities, although I discovered that later in the afternoon she generally retired to her room with a glass of her hot 'toddy' or 'medicine'. I was careful at those times to be tactful and acquiescent, eating my meals and drinking her broth and various concoctions with appeared relish, because once I had gained her trust in my 'good behaviour' I knew the easier it would be to make a temporary escape from captivity. In spite of the unnatural condition in that odious place, the keener my brain seemed to work in a cunning way. Although I could not look back my capacity to plan and look ahead developed. Any sense of time was at a low ebb of course. I hadn't counted the number of nights and days that had passed, but following that first jaunt out I began to do so. I also was careful to keep a sense of geography about the place alive in my head, and I noticed something I'd not previously been aware of – that always following meals or drinks of Mistress Susannah's tasty broth I became relaxed into a hazy feeling of temporary contentment inducing me to sleep. The stronger I grew – due partially to the physical recovery from my accident, I suppose – the firmer and more sinister my suspicions became that she was deliberately drugging me, and one day after she'd left me with my bowl of 'pick-me-up' soup, I pushed it aside untasted and waited for a convenient moment to dispose of it to a hungry cat that was frequently lurking about the premises.

Then, with my dark wrap around me, I turned the knob of the door, and went through to the landing. At first my exploration of the passages leading past the stairs to the far end of the corridor directly opposite that of the study, was bewildering as well as tricky.

There was a wind that day, and the constant moaning and rattling of the old wood was disconcerting. Showers of thin sand were blown against the few narrow windows; at times I was shocked into standing tense in the shadows against the wall, fearing Silas or his sister had seen me and were on my track. Progress was unnerving. I had no precise knowledge of what I was looking for, except a clue of some kind that might evoke a shred of memory. I noticed also that no moment of time should be wasted. Mistress Susannah's 'siesta' might be short. The hateful Master Silas might suddenly take it in his head to visit the study, although I'd been told earlier that he was sufficiently recovered from his cold to take a service at the village chapel that afternoon.

I trusted this was true. To blunder into him on my journey back to the bedroom would be disastrous – even dangerous perhaps to my life itself. I no longer had the slightest faith at all in any pretence he made of godliness or compassion for other human beings than himself.

I was relieved therefore when I came to an unexpected extremely narrow flight of uncarpeted steps cutting up in a sharp turn near the end of the landing. A sliver of light drifted down from above; I went up cautiously – there were twelve steps, ending in an iron door which was half open. I pushed it gingerly. It grated slightly, but the sound was softened by a thud of breaking waves below and the flurry of sand on the wind.

Inside the musty air was cold. The space was small, rectagonal, with two long panels of windows throwing eerie shadows across the interior. Obviously I was in some sort of tower. I went to the window and looked out. Nothing was clear; all was dimmed by the curtain of driven sand and cloud. When my eyes had become accustomed to the strange light, I glanced round. A telescope, similar to the one in the study, lay by a partially broken iron chest, from which one edge of parchment poked; there was a stool, and in one corner a stack of dusty-looking papers huddled by a seaman's cap and a map. Nothing else. I bent down and pushed the lid of the chest open. The piece of parchment had obviously once been a letter, but much of it had gone and the writing was faded. My heart quickened; I picked it up and stuffed it into the large pocket of my wrap, then glanced down again and saw the photograph. It was a poor impression on a torn piece of old newspaper, but I sensed instinctively that it could be of tremendous importance. I took this also and was about to have a further look when the purposeful tread of approaching heavy footsteps echoed frighteningly from below, dispelling everything in my mind but the urgent need to get away.

And this, I knew seconds later, was impossible.

4

He stood in the doorway confronting me. His eyes blazed.

'What the devil does this mean?'

I forced myself to face him boldly, although my pulses hammered painfully.

'I was only looking around.'

He stepped forward. 'Who gave you permission?'

'No one. I – I'm so tired of being cooped up.'

'And you thought "being cooped up" as you call it gave you the right to trespass on other people's premises and privacy poking your audacious little nose into their business?'

'No – I – I—' I broke off, knowing that was precisely what I had been doing.

He took me by the shoulders, shook me and bent his face close to mine. By then I was trembling, but not only through fear.

'I warned you, didn't I?' he said with a certain thickness in his voice that betrayed something else besides anger. 'I told you what a naughty girl could expect who disobeyed. And you're rather more than that, aren't you? A wife! Answer me or I'll – I'll – God help me girl! Don't look like that!' He pulled me to him suddenly and forced his lips on my own, one hand crushing and coursing down my spine and buttocks, pausing a moment, then releasing me with a muttered oath under his breath. He jerked me away, flinging the tumbled wrap at my feet. 'Put that on, and don't let me catch you prowling round again, or by heaven you'll suffer for it, and not by kisses or words.'

I obeyed, mechanically but with a rising niggle of triumph. I shook the hair back from my shoulders, and a moment or two later I was being hustled down the steps to the warren of landings which threaded eventually back to the bedroom.

By then a veneer of composure had been recovered between us.

After pushing me inside the room he said coldly, 'It was a good thing Mistress Susannah was not around. Heaven knows what excuse I could have made for you. But for that matter, you damned well didn't deserve one.'

'I'm sorry,' I told him half-mockingly.

'No you're not. But you will be the next time. Let's hope for your sake there isn't one.'

I didn't answer.

He gave his short ironical laugh, remarking '*Women!*' before turning and leaving, closing the door firmly behind him.

I waited for a time before taking out the papers from my wrap pocket to peruse them.

First of all the dusty newspaper with the image on it. It was so faded and wrinkled that it was impossible to see the features clearly, but a niggle of familiarity stirred me – not exactly of recognition – but tormenting the darkness of amnesia with some kind of indistinctive message that said, this is of great importance to you. Think! *Think!*

I pressed both hands to my temples and tried. But all that consciously registered from the blurred imprint was like that of a mask – the masked face of an elderly gentleman with spots of darkness that could have been eyes above the vague outlines of a nose and jaw fading into the shadow of a beard.

I pushed the paper aside and picked up the letter.

Glancing down at it my whole being seemed to lurch, and after a jerk of the heart a stab of memory that could have been either that of a dream or reality came to life.

Because of the signature.

Jeremiah.

Jeremiah Teale.

Shaking, I managed to decipher the faint but still bold handwriting. Only a portion of the note was there; there was no heading nor an address, but the remaining portion ran – *my bailiff Silas Trevanion tells me he has not yet received my dues. I must warn you, dear sir, that unless I receive these by postilion during the next few days I shall be forced to—* The parchment had been torn at this point leaving only a name below; but what I had read obviously provided the clue I'd been searching for. Like a door being slowly turned in a grating rusty lock, my mind took its first step into the abyss of the past.

Jeremiah Teale.

Very slowly, following a shock of recognition, the warm blood coursed up my spine, spreading its flame to my cheeks and forehead as sweat broke out over my whole body.

Teale had been my name – Isabella Teale. I was not married – nor ever had been – to Justin Llarne. Then who was Jeremiah? And why was I marooned under threat in the wilds of nowhere? How long it was before further threads of memory came into place I do not know. The impact of relief – of being able to recall anything of the past – however disturbing, was at first too patchy to make sense. I sat on the bed and glanced down again at the newspaper cutting showing the blurred photograph lying on the floor. Despite the niggling dim sense of familiarity nothing more concrete registered. And yet the name meant so much.

But what? *What?*

Unfortunately, the more my mind struggled against the miasma of the past the more clouded any feasible explanation became. 'Jeremiah' was the only link, 'Jeremiah', and Teale my own name. There must be a relationship somewhere, but I had no facts yet with which to confront Mistress Susannah and Master Silas.

Ah. Master Silas. According to the torn letter he must once have been bailiff to the author of the script. Then why should he be living in this immense neglected mansion, acting as a professed teacher of religion to the surrounding district?

The whole situation revolved more and more into that

of some carefully planned plot or fairy-tale, but very gradually my mind registered the sinister quality of my own position.

I knew I had to escape as soon as possible; but how and where to?

The huddled hamlet on the moor that I'd glimpsed on rare occasions might be united in the Trevanions' favour and perhaps dangerous for me to visit. I had no precise idea of my locality. The only placename that had been mentioned to me was Falk. My supposed former home.

Although my mind boggled at the constant run of conflicting thoughts the past was clear; without Mistress Susannah's concoctions my brain was gradually able to function and question in a comparatively reasonable manner.

The result might be terrifying, but I had to use all the cunning I had in finding a way through the well of intrigue to enlightenment and sanity.

It was my sanity, obviously, that Mistress Susannah was doing her best to destroy.

I had a feeling there was little time to waste, and on the first opportunity the following day I contrived to escape unseen, and reach the gate in the courtyard from where the track wound in a thin ribbon-like line to the jagged point bordering Falk.

A veil of mist hugged the calm water and treacherous coast. Suppressed fear not only of pursuit, but of taking a false step that could send me plunging to my death stiffened my muscles and alerted my senses to every slight sound – the cracking of a twig, the rhythm of breaking waves below, the rustle of some small wild creature

through the undergrowth and the sudden high squawking of a gull. Even the pumping of my heart against
eardrums held a similar warning of danger.

The way was rough and prickly. More than once my
cloak was caught by a gorse bush or bramble halting me
for precious seconds while I managed to get untangled. At
one point, when the light thickened, I made a reckless
jump over what I supposed was a pool or bog, and when I
looked back as the mist lifted discovered it was no pool at
all, but a sheer precipitous cut in the rock which if I had
not cleared it would have sent me plunging to my death
hundreds of feet below.

I waited for minutes to recover from the shock, then
went on again making sure the direction was inland rather
than seawards.

Then, quite suddenly, the path took a gentler slope
down; the undergrowth thinned, giving a more clarified
view of what lay ahead. I was nearer Falk than I'd
expected; round the curved point of the coast the house
with the chimney stood massive and grey with its grounds
sloping abruptly downwards over what appeared to be a
narrow cove. I continued carefully along the track while
negotiating with care the ascent that steepened again,
ending abruptly on a damp shadowed stretch of beach.

I stood for several minutes on the wet sand peering
through damp lashes round the cavernous scene of
humped rock and granite stones grouped witch-like
beneath an overhang of cliff. Lifting my head I could
perceive just the tip of the tall chimney, but the main
structure of the building was lost at such near range. I
moved ahead, startling a wild bird that flew squawking to

the grey sea. It was difficult in the uncertain light to discern exactly what was real and what illusion. Shadows hugged small caves and inlets of the rough coast; but as a flurry of wind took a swirl of foggy air away the scene was momentarily clarified. I had already turned the point, and saw the humped silhouette of a boat that looked like a lugger moored in by a sharp inlet only a hundred yards or so away.

The very stillness was menacing, emphasizing the strange sense of wandering through a mirage of unreality – all the more frightening because I knew myself to be real enough. The trickle of blood down my forehead and arm where brambles or thorns had scratched it was warm and painful. I put a handkerchief to my face, and pressed ahead until I came upon a hole of darkness cutting into the rock. I thought at first it must merely be another natural cave. But when I drew close and bent forward for a proper look I saw it was more than that. In spite of the mist that curled and writhed in flimsy veils of salty air, the structure was obviously that of some man-made passage. It could have been at one time the work of nature, but the walls, lunging in parts, were black and shining, tunnelling into the bowels of the earth above.

I went in, and the space widened. There was a dank strange smell about it, redolent with something more pungent than sea and sand.

What?

At a sudden curve I stood still, staring.

A thin beam of light showed me I was in some kind of room – well, not a room exactly, but a sort of cellar; and I was not alone. Ahead of me, motionless, but sinister looking against the background of contorted shadows, Jed's pale face emerged like that of some grotesque clown.

Jed.

His heavy features were caught sideways in a pale radiance streaming from behind. After a brief pause in which he glared unsmilingly without movement, I forced myself towards him, and was caught in a beam of brighter light that revealed a sudden turn in the macabre interior.

Then I stopped again, astonished.

All manner of objects were huddled in a heap at the far end. The glitter of what appeared to be jewels and silver, intermingled with *objets d'art*, pieces of sculpture, carvings, rugs and ancient furnishings, all lit to eerie brilliance from what was obviously a door slightly ajar in the ceiling. And at one side, propped against a rock, was a painting. The portrait of a woman – pale, fine-featured, with massed silver-gold hair. Just for a second her beauty seemed to dominate the whole scene. My heart beat painfully against my ribs. Could this be real, I wondered, or was I dreaming again? Was the experience just part of the continued nightmare of amnesia? But when Jed spoke I knew it wasn't. It was real enough.

'Hullo,' he said. He didn't smile, just stood there, with his small piggy eyes watchful and intense upon me.

I knew instinctively I must not show fear. If I did anything might happen. So I had to be nice to him, appease him for my sudden appearance. I forced a smile and answered with brittle false brightness, 'Hullo, Jed. How – how nice to see you, I didn't expect to find a friend here. And – and you're a *friend*, aren't you—?'

I broke off waiting. For seconds there was no response.

The stillness of the bulky form was itself more frightening than any movement would have been. He had the grotesque quality of one of the stone gargoyles come to life.

'It's all right,' I continued, 'I'm – I shan't hurt you, Jed. I *like* you.' Oh, what a lie! but an intuitive cunning – fears for my own safety, drove me to it. 'And you like me, don't you—?'

Suddenly he smiled – a grin of the thick lips that stretched from ear to ear. The large head nodded vigorously. He stepped forward with a flabby hand extended. I took it, trying not to shudder at the cold impact of what felt like a wet fish. His head was still bobbing backwards and forwards when I managed to pull my arm away and put a finger to my lips conspiratorily.

'We mustn't say anything,' I told him. 'This is a secret, isn't it? A *secret* between you and me. *Your* secret, yours and mine?'

'Secret!' he echoed. 'Ais. Secret; you'n me – eh?'

'Just us two, Jed. No one else. No one at all.'

He nodded again vigorously. 'You an' me.'

'That's right, that's right.'

When he still stood there I continued, with the desperate hope his mood wouldn't suddenly change, 'You go now and say nothing. Don't tell *anyone*.'

He copied me by putting a chubby finger to his mouth, then moved, pushed past me, and like some ungainly creature of the wilds hobbled away and disappeared down the tunnel of mist through the mouth of the holed cave into the darkness.

I glanced round, and peered at the portrait. It was

unframed and had a crack across it. The edges of the canvas were frayed and torn, but the exquisite features were unimpaired, and startlingly pale against the dripping dank walls. It was impossible to detect any expression on the proud face, but a glint of green in the shaft of light striking downwards from the door gave the uncanny impression of cat-like contempt that was unnerving. As I passed I imagined for a second that a faint tinkle of shrill laughter pierced the stillness. But it was only a slither of a pebble when my toe caught it.

Overhead the ceiling sloped down considerably and before me a blank wall of granite blocked further exploration. Everywhere treasures of some kind or another were heaped. I found that if I stood on a flat lump of stone I could reach the ceiling from where the thin light trickled. It was cold, but of wood, and firmly wedged.

A *trap* door.

I was about to give a vigorous push when it suddenly opened. I lost my balance and fell back. The next moment a strong figure jumped down almost landing on top of me.

Like the crack of a whip an oath shattered the air explosively, and a strong hand grasped my cloak near the chin, dragging me up, half strangling me.

Justin's face with blazing eyes and set mouth above a disordered cravat eyed me furiously.

'What the devil are you doing now?' he said. 'I warned you, didn't I—'

I managed to wrench myself free. 'If you touch me I'll – I'll—'

He threw back his head and laughed, but it was not a pleasant sound. I waited, wondering wildly what to do –

whether to brazen things out and risk confronting him, or run, but knew the latter would be useless. I sensed that despite his strong frame he would be fleet as a fox in pursuit. And then – I shivered in a tumult of mixed emotions – terror, anger, humiliation and a strange primitive kind of physical pleasure.

Quite suddenly the laughter died. With his bold head thrust forward, his stern gaze firmly upon me, he continued, 'Well, you would *what*, madam? Speak up. A simple question, I'd have thought, for a nimble brain like yours.'

'I want your help,' I told him. 'There's no one else. You say you're my husband. If you are, isn't it your *duty*—'

'*Duty*? To *what*?'

'To get me out of that dreadful place,' I cried in a torrent of words. 'They're *drugging* me! *She* is, anyway, Mistress Susannah. I know. I *know*. She *wants* me to forget. She puts stuff in my food; every time I start to remember—'

'Oh.' His voice was sharp. 'So you *are* remembering.'

'Only little things – like "Jeremiah". I remember the name. And I had a dream, a nightmare, and – and—' I broke off helplessly. There was a pause, and when he didn't speak, I began again. 'I suppose it's no good. You don't believe me.'

To my astonishment he answered thoughtfully, in strangely altered tones, 'Many wouldn't, but maybe I do.'

'Then—' I moved towards him eagerly, but he put up a hand with a recovery of his former mood, and said sharply, 'Don't take it for granted because I'm fool enough to be swayed by your pretty face, and show of words which could be play-acting for all I know – that you have

me by the ears, madam. Truth to tell, it will be something
to have another pair of hands about to do a bit of work,
providing they stay out of mischief, and keep out of sight
of the Trevanions. Understand?'

'Yes, yes,' I told him, though I didn't, quite. 'Anything
you say.'

'Hm!'

He made some curt comment, took one quick look
round the dark interior, and grasped my arm so firmly I
winced.

'Come along then.'

A short large ladder swung snake-like from above. He
pulled me towards it, mounted it himself with the speed of
an athlete, and clambered through.

'Up with you,' he shouted. 'It's only a few steps. Take
those frilly things off – cloak and skirt. Here's my hand.
Gadzooks, girl! – frightened?'

Angered that he could think me such a poor creature, I
did just what he said, and eventually, aided by his strong
right arm, arrived intact but embarrassed in what was
presumably the cellar of Falk. Barrels were stacked in one
corner, and numerous bottles on shelves. Justin let the
door fall to with a thud. The heavy smell of malt mingled
with spirits and damp penetrated the atmosphere. I felt
foolish standing there in the ungainly pantaloons inflicted
on me by Mistress Susannah. I'd thrown my cloak up to
him, but the skirt had fallen, and the bodice of my dress
had ripped on a nail, revealing a glimpse of bare skin
above the corsets.

I stared at him mutinously.

'What about my clothes?'

He grinned. 'Oh, don't worry, there are plenty of breeches around to protect your virginity, and I'm sure you'll find those better for working in here than those trumpery falals of Mistress Susannah's.'

'*Breeches?*' I gasped.

'Why not, Mrs Llarne. Since you insist on meddling in male affairs it's fitting surely for you to dress like one.'

'For *you* perhaps. But—'

'*And* for you, I can assure you. Didn't I make it clear I didn't intend to house and protect you for nothing? Since your – accident – you've had enough time to laze about. My man, Joel, needs assistance in doing what has to be done in this place. He's getting old and if you can help him when he needs a hand in scrubbing a floor, or raking out a stove or preparing a meal, I expect you to do it as willingly as any young cub paid in silver for the job.'

'A sort of scullion,' I said coldly.

'Or you could say a wilful imp of a wife needing a good lesson.'

I looked away, not wishing him to see the flush on my face.

'You've put things very clearly,' I told him.

'It's important you should know your position exactly in this house,' he commented.

I turned and gave him an icy little smile. 'Presumably I must have known it better in the past when I was legally its mistress – if I ever was.'

'Ah! But then you don't remember, do you?'

I decided to play with him.

'But you don't know that. Suppose things were coming back to me now? Suppose I know more about everything –

than you believe. It could be, couldn't it?'

He took my chin between his two strong hands and stared straight and deep into my eyes. I tried to calm my quickened breathing, but my heart thumped into my ears.

'If you deceive me,' he said, 'you'll regret it – in more ways than one.'

A little shiver ran down my spine.

My defences fell.

'I shan't deceive you. And this old man, Joel – I'll do what I can to be of assistance.'

He let me go.

'He isn't that old, and his first thought always is to do what I require of him like keeping an eye on you. You'll not wander away from Falk for instance. That's important. To show yourself in the village could be dangerous.'

I sighed. 'Oh, how I wish you'd tell me the truth – *all* of it, what I'm doing here, why I must remain unseen. The mystery of those things down below in the cave. And the painting of that woman—' I broke off, knowing from the dark look on his face that I'd made a mistake in commenting on the portrait.

'The picture has nothing to do with you,' he said sharply. 'So keep your pretty mouth shut, and put this on' – he took a coarse kind of sack-cloth from a peg, and flung it at me – 'before I'm tempted to teach you a lesson of manners in an extremely undignified fashion – for you.'

I wrapped it round me hastily.

He was smiling slightly again. Just for a moment I disliked him intensely – his bravado, self-confidence, and power over me. Although I sensed that his threats were partially at least for effect, the result was disturbing and disruptive to any possible chance of normal friendship between us. What part did he play in the macabre set of circumstances enveloping me, I wondered, not for the first time? And which was the *real* Justin? The colourful individual acting the role of bullying husband? Or the more understanding stranger glimpsed in rare moments willing to lend a helpful hand to me in my plight?

There was simply no guide to the answer. I had to act as wisely as I could and go blindly along with him when necessary, trusting that in time something would either jerk my memory to life, or facts emerge day by day providing the vital answer to the puzzle. The latter was most probable, I thought, especially as the sinister effect of Mistress Susannah's drugging gradually wore off.

I was pulled from my brief daze of conjecturing by Justin ordering me to follow him up a flight of stone steps to a door at the far end of the cellar. He pushed me through into a flagged passage. From there we entered the kitchen quarters, a vast terrain consisting of a wide ill-lit interior with smaller pantries and a scullery leading off. There was a long table in the centre and a fire burning from a large stove in an alcove. A man was crouched on a stool with his hands to the flames. He looked up as we approached. His face was lined and scarred, the chin long with a grizzle of beard on it under a hooked nose. Not at all welcoming.

'Joel!' Justin said to me. And to the man. 'We have a visitor. Company to do a fair share of work when necessary. She can sleep in cook's old room. And it will be your business to see no one knows of a *woman's* presence. The name's Kim.' As though remembering something, he added, 'I'm in no mood to be fettered by a wife's moods and megrims. Understand?'

Joel nodded, giving an affirmative grunt.

My impression of being in a macabre fairy-tale or dream intensified as I followed Joel up a short flight of back stairs to a small room that must once have been comfortable but was now in a state of disuse and neglect, slightly steamy from the elements outside, and heat from kitchens below. There were two windows, washstand, wardrobe, chest, a brass bed in one corner, with a round table beside it, and a shabby armchair pushed close to a small fireplace; there were few indications that any feminine presence had ever graced its dusty interior – just an old slipper near the wardrobe, and a lace cap more grey than white hanging from a peg. As I glanced at this Justin pulled it down. 'You'll not be needing this,' he said curtly. 'Caps don't go with breeches, and when that mane comes off you'll not be needing it.'

I was startled and instinctively a hand went to my hair. 'What do you mean?'

'Nothing to harm your health,' he answered airily. 'Just a precaution, in case you take it in your head ever to show yourself when you shouldn't – from a window perhaps, or slip up out on to the moors. A good clip or two with a strong pair of scissors should do the trick adequately.'

I stared at him until the meaning of his words fully sank in. Then I said, almost unbelievingly, 'Cut off my hair, is that what you want? But why – *why*?'

'That's my business,' he answered curtly, adding a little more gently, 'You wanted my help. I'm giving it – to the new youth in my employment – *Kim*.'

'But *why*?' I asked in desperation.

He sighed and his jaw hardened again. 'Have you done with your questions? One day, if you act wisely and do as you're told, you'll know. You have my word for it.'

I had to believe him and, despite his arrogance, I did.

Looking back now, my memories – and how marvellous it is to use the word again without fear – are a medley of mixed experiences and confused emotions which register now in a panorama of exciting incidents involving the history and bitter heritage of Falk.

In spite of Justin's prediction of hard work, I found little to do except clean round and about the certain back areas of the house where I was allowed to go, and in the kitchen. Joel from the first resented my intrusion in a place where he had learned to consider himself sole guardian, although he did his best not to show it, being wary of giving offence to his master. For a few days after my arrival there my tasks were mostly in preparing vegetables for the main meal – generally stew – that was taken at night.

The three of us ate at the long trestle table in the kitchen, a silent unsociable meal, although on two occasions Justin was absent. Joel seemed edgy then; a little nerve by one temple flickered, his small eyes watchful, constantly upon me, and I could sense his ears were alert for a sign of some signal to action that was mystifying. I had expected life to be simpler at the house with the chimney than with the domineering Trevanions, but although fractions of memories from the past rose to the surface of my mind at rare intervals, they as quickly died, leaving me more-than-ever puzzled by my own existence and past.

Being made to dress like a youth didn't help. Justin had himself cropped my hair and provided me with a short chocolate-coloured cloth coat, cream shirt and cravat, fawn knee breeches and thick stockings, and told me grudgingly that I made a pert, engaging enough boy.

'But don't take advantage of it,' he said when he saw me thus. 'No sly chit-chat to Polly when she comes – Polly's a girl I have from a farm nearby on certain days to do what work's neessary. Keep away from her or you may find my riding crop about you.'

Because I was becoming accustomed to his threats I'd said recklessly, 'You needn't worry. I'm not interested in any Polly. But you needn't bully. There's no need to threaten. You're not that kind of person, anyway – not really.'

We were standing at the foot of the short staircase to my room.

'How do you know?'

In a stray beam of light from a nearby oil lamp I saw the hard lines of his face soften, and realized in a strange moment of awareness how stirringly handsome under different, gentler circumstances he could be.

I shrugged. Perhaps I smiled slightly. I don't know. A moment of silence had followed between us holding an indefinable communion, an awareness of unseen, unplumbed longing that held us briefly bound beyond all physical conditions.

Then his arm was round me. His firm lips on my cheek. I'd pressed close thrilled by the warmth. But the spell broke suddenly. He'd drawn away, straightened up, turned, and not looking at me, said, 'None of that. You're hired as a servant, not a mistress.'

I put my hand to my burning hot cheek. 'Thank you. I'm very much obliged.'

Forgetting my male outfit, I made a gesture to lift my skirt daintily above my toes in the manner of a lady, before moving quickly up the stairs. Realizing my stupidity, I ran two steps at a time, not wishing to hear his derisive laughter. But I don't think he laughed. Only the echo of his footsteps gradually receded down the hall, followed by the slam of a door.

Then he was gone.

Once safely – if that is the right word to use – in the bedroom, I turned the key in the lock – one favour granted to me in this strange new abode – and flopped on to the bed, and made an attempt to relax. A maze of questions raced through my brain. I meant to keep my promise to Justin in keeping out of sight of Mistress Susannah and Master Silas – but would Jed keep his word not to divulge having met me in the cave? And why had Justin appeared so disturbed concerning my mention of the woman's portrait? Obviously the collection of treasures was in one way connected with illegal dealing and his business with Silas, which was partly why he had been so intent on keeping my presence at Falk secret from him by disguising me as a boy. But if by some chance I *was* seen, would the camouflage work? A number of other queries followed, none of them with answers that made sense.

Presently, when I'd regained my breath, I went to the mirror and took a good look at the reflection. I saw a slim, youthful, figure with pert features – wide eyes, short nose in a heart-shaped face, that had a fey look in the half-light. Me, and yet *not* me, but rather like some bygone youth from a Shakespearean play. And again – who was I? but I knew that, didn't I? I'd remembered.

Isabella Teale.

Suddenly the knowledge swept through me again – a challenge from the past, heralding recognition. One truth registered. I might lack full memory, but I had identity.

I jerked myself to move and went to the small side window.

It was early evening shortly following the night meal. In the creek beyond the cove the vessel I'd sighted earlier was moving out to sea, a dark shape with four-cornered sails. At the same time there was a stirring in the water of smaller vessels. A figure emerged from the shadows, head thrust forward, like a giant carrion crow's, and stood for a few moments before turning and receding once more into the thin gathering mist. The resemblance to Master Silas could have been merely a figment of my imagination, and probably was. But I waited there, peering through the foam-blurred glass, sensing more was to come. When five minutes or so later it did, the event was apparently unimportant – just a small craft setting out, possibly on a night's fishing.

Everything was very quiet. Only the steady breaking of waves on the rocks below, and a night bird's cry. Presently, feeling chilled and tired I went to my bed. And that night the name 'Jeremiah' once more haunted my dreams.

* * *

During the next few days as my dazed state clarified to an approaching sense of reality, I tried to assess the passing of time and how long it was since the fateful happening that had sent me plunging into the well of oblivion through the dark porch guarded by the great gargoyles. It was still as though a shutter fell, blocking out time and any means to a logical answer. My only comfort was that Justin had accepted my assertion concerning the effort of Mistress Susannah's insidious brews and drugging. I couldn't help admitting to myself that *he* also had been acting strangely, especially in his determination to change me into a boy. But beneath my doubts and problemizing lingered a deep sense that he had justification, and that fundamentally he was on my side. All I had to do, all I *could* do, was to try and trust him and wait. Following this knowledge, a message to myself was born and developed in my mind. And the message was – 'You are Isabella Teale. You must have been on some mission. And the mission will be clear when the proper time arrives'.

But how long would that time be?

I was at work in the kitchen one day in the absence of Joel who was doing something outside concerning Justin's fishing boat, when Justin himself came in and said, 'Glad to see you busy. But stop all that for the moment. I want to talk to you.'

I took my wet hands from the sink, dried them, pushed a lock of hair from one temple, turned and answered, 'Well. I'm here. What is it?'

He was staring at me enigmatically, looking very handsome in fawn silk, narrow breeches and pointed-toed black boots, a tailed rust-coloured fitted velveteen coat and embroidered waistcoat, with a jewelled pin in the neck scarf encircling the high white collar .

'You don't sound very pleased.'

'Should I be?'

He shrugged. 'Perhaps not. But I'm not about to chide you. Odd as it may seem, I have a request.'

I could feel my eyes widen. 'A *request*? You?'

'It may seem devilish peculiar considering the way I've had to keep you in your place. But odd's fish! However else could a hot-blooded male deal with a wilful hussy like you?'

I didn't answer, but could feel my cheeks burning, though I managed to keep my gaze unflinchingly under his.

Then he briefly looked away, walked to the door, turned, came back to face me, and said, 'For one evening I want you to rid yourself of breeches and be your own tantalizing self again. You'll find a gown waiting for you upstairs on the bed, with a few of the unmentionable frillies women wear. May not be exactly up-to-date, but suitable enough for this out-of-the-way place—'

I tried to speak, but he put a hand up warningly. 'Hold your tongue until I've finished. I've a friend visiting me this evening who'll expect to meet my wife. Nothing to worry about – for you. Only a glimpse will be necessary. You'll be in the garden room – sniffing a posy of some sort, all feminine elegance and grace, or lounging on the settee with smelling salts to your wicked little nose. Anyway, I've no doubt you know all the tricks, and when I arrive on that pleasant little romantic scene with my crony, you'll get up gracefully and offer your hand – there'll be mittens for you upstairs – while I say, "My wife, Captain Fitzgerald". No doubt he'll kiss your fingertips, which is the fashion I believe these days.' There was a short pause while I tried to get my thoughts under control. 'Will you do it?' he asked after a few moments.

'But – my hair. How could I appear at *all* feminine with – with no hair to powder or arrange? I'd look just ridiculous.'

He drew close to me, so close I could feel his warm breath on my face, put both hands on my shoulders, surveyed me as though contemplating some commercial project, then smiled and ruffled the short curls.

'Oh, I think the effect will be quite devastating,' he said. 'I'm not well versed in female fashions these days, but with charm like yours fashions don't matter a damn. A full-blooded man's far more concerned with other things.'

'You mean you want me to – to *charm* him? Are you trying to get rid of me? Is that what you intend – for me to – to – to *seduce* him?'

'No, by Gad, it isn't. Here you are and here you'll stay if I have to keep you here by the scruff of your pretty neck.'

'By force,' I said, the anger rising in me again. 'Just like it was with the Trevanions? The same situation all over again.'

He shook his head slowly. 'No, it isn't the same at all,' he replied in softened tones. 'You're here, I hope – through choice partly. Isn't that true?'

Suddenly resistance died in me. I said nothing, because I had no chance. His kiss was warm and demanding on my lips. I could feel his heart thudding through the thick velvet of his coat. For a delirious few seconds everything else faded and I knew only sweetness in a delirium of delight. Then he drew away, straightened his cravat, and said, 'So! – we must forget this now and get on with the business. I take it all is arranged. Be ready by six o'clock. You have a clock in your room now. Joel or myself will arrive to take you down when the time comes.'

A minute later he had left the kitchen and gone out by a side door, leaving me to contemplate and arrange the evening ahead.

The dress left on my bed was not strictly for evening, but an elegant gown in pale-green satin, with a fitted bodice, a high lacy neckline and spreading full skirt bunched at the back with tiny bows. The sleeves were full, but caught into tight lace cuffs.

Was it fashionable? Or out of date? I didn't know. But its richness and style awed me. So presumably from the back of memory instinct told me I had not been used to such luxury, and I seemed to recall from those forgotten days a necessity for economy. If that was true the fact more than ever dispelled the assertion that I was, or ever had been, married to Justin. Or did it? What I had seen in brief glimpses of the house with the chimney though indicative of past elegance had suggested extreme neglect. On the day following my arrival Justin had given me a cursory glance of private apartments, and had therefore forbidden them to me. I'd been dimly conscious of a wide flagged hall and staircase and half-open doors revealing vast rooms, one in particular with chandeliers hanging from a high ornately encrusted ceiling. But the impression had been dimmed by dust, and at one point a cobweb had brushed my face.

'This part of Falk is mostly shut now,' Justin had told me. 'Open only occasionally when there's entertaining to do, and Joel and Polly have a good clean round then. *Your* services will not be required here, so see you keep to the back quarters. That's an order.'

I'd agreed, and had been relieved to return to the comparative warmth of the kitchen, away from the musty odour of old tapestries, worn hangings and damp walls where heavy framed portraits stared like condemning ghosts from the shadows.

Now, however, despite Justin's former injunctions, I was not only to be *allowed* – but had been *requested* to make an appearance in the forbidden premises.

Titillated by the knowledge, I held the dress in front of me, surveyed as much of myself as was possible through the oval mirror hanging above the dressing-table. The space was limited, and the glass surface cracked at one corner. Obviously the 'cook' alluded to by Justin hadn't bothered about her looks. She'd probably been a plain woman, or old. But the limited vision confronting me was neither. The colour suited me, giving light to my eyes which seemed to reflect varied shades of translucent hazel flecked with green and gold. High cheekbones were faintly shadowed by thick black lashes, and my mouth tilted above a small pointed chin. Not exactly beautiful, but pleasing somehow, and what Justin had said was true, the short curling mop of hair had a certain feminine allure that could have been enhanced if I had a flower or ribbon to entwine and stick in it. But I had none: just the dress and frilly underwear packed into a flat box.

I wondered where Justin had got them. They might be

old, but obviously were unused – unlike the gown presented to me by Mistress Susannah for my first interview with Master Silas and Justin.

Trying to get the bewildering past events into proper consecutive order was really quite disorientating; but in those few moments of viewing the dress, one fact registered clearly – in some obscure way the *real* me now had a link with the history of both places – Falk, and the grim mansion behind the porch of the gargoyles. The two houses were connected, and that evening I was to meet a further character in the curious drama of my present existence – Captain Fitzgerald.

5

The garden room led from the dining-room which was next to the library. I knew that because as Joel guided me down the main hall, I glimpsed through a half-open door walls of books and caught a whiff of cigar smoke. Both those interiors emitted a subtle sense of being lived in recently and were less neglected than the rest of that vast interior.

The small place I was shown into must have been at the side of the house and looked over a patch of wind-blown land cultivated behind a granite wall. A few tired-looking chrysanthemums still bloomed wanly from a border, but most of the space was thick with the twisted trunks of rhododendron bushes. There was no glimpse of the sea; and no fireplace, but the air was very warm, and had been cunningly devised somehow, I guessed, through unseen pipes from the kitchen quarters. How had I any knowledge of such things, I wondered, when Joel had left me? Was it that I'd been employed in a kitchen sometime in my past life? Or was I just imagining and conjecturing? I didn't *feel* as though I'd been a servant. But – oh! there were so many 'buts'. Every time I tried to think back I became more than ever confused.

The furnishing of the small room was simple. One or two spindle-backed chairs, a small pedestal table, and a leather settee. The floor was covered by oilcloth and rugs that must once have been rich and colourful but were now worn and shabby. On a shelf near the window a few hothouse exotic plants were in bloom.

I remembered Justin's suggestion that I should be sniffing a posy when Captain Fitzgerald arrived. The idea now seemed quite ridiculous. The poor blossoms looked droopy and were obviously in need of water. However, with a quirk of humour I decided I might manage to drape myself swathed in the green satin on the shabby settee, in a manner calculated to give a touch of exotic grace to the scene.

The difficulty was in not knowing how long it would be before the two men appeared. It might be quite soon, or possibly an hour during which time my muscles and nerves would grow tense from waiting.

Actually little more than fifteen minutes must have passed before the sound of men's voices and footsteps echoed from the hall. A moment or two later the dining-room door opened, followed by that of the small sanctum where I'd hurriedly arranged myself and my luxurious skirt over the leather upholstered settee.

'My dear—' Justin said coming forward, 'this is Captain

Fitzgerald.' He ushered his companion forward. 'Meet my wife, sir.'

Having got to my feet with as much dignity as I could muster, I lifted a mittened hand to his lace-edged cuffed one. He was very gallant and bent his head letting his lips briefly touch my fingertips.

'Pleased to meet you, ma'am,' he said in cultured tones. I'd expected a captain to be wearing uniform; but the man before me was attired in clothes of a sombre tone, embellished by a cream cravat with diamond tie-pin, and jewelled cufflinks suggesting he was a man of substance, probably a country squire, rather than of some military status.

The meeting between us was brief, including such mundane topics as the weather, life in the country as opposed to that in London – of which I knew nothing – the recent steam and rail achievements of Brunel, and a reference for my benefit obviously, to the change in women's fashions during the last decade from the Empire to Victorian style, of which the captain said he highly approved, with a complimentary glance at my green satin.

I did my best to appear intelligent with the very minimum of words. Whether I succeeded or not, I never knew, because the finale of the conversation came as a shock.

'My dear lady,' the captain was saying, 'it has been delightful meeting you, and I hope one day to do so again. But alas! I have to be gone now. Time passes all too quickly and I have to call at Carnwikken to see old Jeremiah Teale—'

The world swam round me. I recall vaguely his bowing,

and the touch of his hand once more on my own. The two figures faded, then all became blurred, until a sharp pain stabbed from the top of my head through my brain and everything was suddenly clear.

I remembered.

It is strange how the combination of a few words can bring the sleeping mind to sudden vivid consciousness. With me the name 'Carnwikken' in conjunction with 'Jeremiah Teale' had the magic impact.

In one vivid second the curtain of the forgotten past was shattered and I was seeing my mother's thin face white against the pillows as she lay dying.

'You must go to Carnwikken,' she'd managed to say. 'Find your Great Uncle Jeremiah. You're his only kin now. When I'm gone this family feud will be over. Remember, Isabella – Jeremiah Teale, *Carnwikken*, near Treeve, Cornwall. He'll tell you what to do – I've left a little for you in the bank, but—' She'd tried to say more, but had failed. A moment or two later she was gone, leaving me alone in the world to face the grief of her loss and an unknown future ahead.

In those first moments of recollection following Captain Fitzgerald's remark a whole panorama of events flashed from the past to the present. I saw myself as one sometimes does in a dream, setting off to do her bidding after her humble funeral. Then the long tiring journey by coach and rail train from Bristol to Cornwall to find Great Uncle Jeremiah. I recalled walking with my valise along a moorland road and asking the way to Carnwikken from a stranger on a horse. I hadn't seen his face clearly. He'd lifted an arm and directed me along a high track cutting in an opposite direction from the nearby hamlet I'd been aiming for. This was a curving lane facing the horizon of tumpy hills. I'd taken it feeling very wearied, and at last reached the house with the gargoyle porch.

Then something had hit me. I'd not stumbled or fallen accidentally.

I'd been attacked.

Attacked.

Pulling myself from past to present, I found myself in the hall of Falk, with Justin staring down on me. Something was stinging my throat.

'Better?' he queried.

I nodded, feeling the colour rise in my cold cheeks. 'It was the shock. Everything came back to me. When your friend said Carnwikken, I knew. I'm *not* your wife: I never was. I'm Isabella Teale. And—'

He interrupted me by reaching for a brandy flask from the table and pouring more.

'Take this,' he told me, forcing it upon me. 'And you mustn't explain. I know all that's necessary.'

I swallowed; more of a gulp. 'Then why—'

'Let the explaining rest for a bit,' he retorted peremptorily. 'We'll get you to your room now, before Joel gets back from the stables. Can you walk? Or shall I carry you?'

I rose to my feet defiantly, feeling light-headed and a bit shaky. 'I'm quite capable.'

'I'm sure you are. But you need to lie down for a bit.'

He accompanied me to the bedroom, wanting to take my arm which I resisted, with a show of bravado.

Once there he turned to leave and was about to close the door when I cried impetuously, 'Justin – Mr Llarne, haven't I a right to know *now*? You must know how I came here – how I was hit and knocked unconscious in the doorway of the house – Carnwikken – and held prisoner by the awful Trevanions? And my uncle – my Great Uncle Jeremiah, where is he? I've come all the way from Bristol. Did you know that? Just to see him, but—'

'Have done, Isabella,' he said using my name for the first time. 'If you must know—' He came to the bed, paused, then continued, 'Your uncle is dead.'

'*Dead*?' I gasped. 'Do you mean killed or something, or—?'

'No, no. He died naturally from pneumonia on top of a chill. He's buried near the back of the house. Later I'll show you the grave. But at the moment try and curb that devil of curiosity in you. I have other things to deal with. Bad things are happening in the world, including a war with China. There's a plot involving Silas and his sister. You shall know everything *when the time comes*. Just hold your tongue, keep yourself out of sight and try to be patient for once in your life. Understand?'

His jaw and expression were so set, his voice so compelling, his gaze so hard upon mine, that I nodded.

'If you say so.'

'I *do* say so. Behave. Act naturally in front of Joel. And remember – I'm your friend.'

'Or your boy servant – Kim? Isn't that how you see me?'

'Both. And more – as the clever woman you are under your provocative façade, and quick-witted enough to know what's good for you.'

I sighed. 'How long will it go on? The pretending and hiding and waiting – *waiting* to know the truth. It sounds so complicated and unreal. And I have a right – *surely* – to hear about my own uncle?' I broke off, watching the relentless mutinous look cross his face again. But there was a touch of softening in his expression too. He bent down unexpectedly and drew me to him. 'Of course you have. And you'll get it, the whole story when I've time to tell it. Now, Isabella,' his voice was gruff against my ear, 'stop tormenting me. Gadzooks, girl! We need all the strength we have – both of us – for what lies ahead. Now have done, for the love of God, this is no time for pretty words and romances. Would you have me a weakling playing woeful ballads while Rome's burning? Would you? *Would* you?'

I struggled against him, but my senses were once more overwhelmed by the pressure of his mouth travelling from my ear down my neck to a shoulder, and when he released me my whole being was on fire. He straightened up, lifted a hand to his face, and took three strides to the door.

'You'd best rest awhile,' he commented curtly before going, 'and give us both a chance for common sense to get working.'

There was a sharp slam and he had gone.

I was bemused, no longer by the strange situation but by him. Yes, I was in the middle of an adventure but it was not the adventure itself that gave me such exhilaration, not even the excitement of recovered memory, but the thrilling awareness that Justin Llarne and myself were in the same world together.

6

The next two days were storm-lashed, with gales sweeping the coast, moaning dismally round the stone walls of Falk, sending rain and spray in a wild tattoo against windows and doors. The kitchen was chill in spite of the fire that Joel kept alight with logs, and I busied myself as much as possible with housework. I saw Justin only at rare intervals, and knew he was pondering on events to come. He appeared almost impersonal and aloof to me, in spite of our past passionate interlude.

On the third day everything changed; the winds died; all was quiet, with every small sound intensified because of a brooding, waiting sense of tension.

'Go to your room and stay there,' Justin told me. 'Don't dare show your saucy face until I say.'

'A prisoner again?'

'For your own good. And don't argue.'

I gave him a wry little half-smile. 'I do my best not to.'

'Hm!' His glance was speculative, half-amused, yet concerned. He turned on his heel saying, 'Be off now. And take heed of what I've said.'

Then he was gone.

The stillness, following the storm, was oppressive. I had nothing to do but lie on my bed, mend a stocking with thread I'd found in a little drawer of the chest, once most probably belonging to cook – and thumb through an old newspaper lying there dated 1834 which made references to Lord Palmerston, the East India Company and Anglo-Chinese trade. Its only interest to me was that Justin had said something to me concerning the Chinese Opium War. But I knew nothing tangible about that, and found the closely printed columns dull and boring. I got up restlessly several times and went to the door listening for some sign of activity. How long it was before it came I couldn't judge, because the little clock I'd been lent had stopped ticking, and the light was perceptibly fading. By then my body was tired through tension, senses keyed to the unmistakable undertone of talking, muffled conversation and the intermittent shuffle of footsteps.

At one point I fancied Silas Trevanion's thin high voice penetrated the rest, and my heart quickened. What was happening now? What sly plot was being hatched? For of a certainty anything that involved Silas must be deep and sly and somehow sickening.

Then all of a sudden the muted sounds ceased. There was the slam of a door, followed by another more distant one, and a medley of disjointed noises that resolved into one indistinct rumble before fading altogether.

Was Joel still about? I didn't know. But I decided to risk Justin's anger if I was discovered, and take a quick glance through the long window which looked out from the short landing joining my room. It had a direct view of the sea and I had a strong feeling of dramatic events approaching that might explode disastrously round the coast of Falk.

I had half expected to see Jed lurking in the shadows when I looked down the corridor, but there was no sign of anyone. I crossed to the window. The Atlantic was grey under a sullen sky, and already a faint mist hugged the horizon. But the scene was sufficiently clear to discern the dark long shape of a fairly large sailing boat apparently motionless on the distant waters.

The complete silence was eerie, almost as though emptiness itself had become an entity, engulfing the house.

I waited there for some time, watching and listening. Presently I heard it again – the low thrum of voices gradually intensifying, accompanied by the thump of boats from somewhere below. There was a curious reverberation of sound – hollow, rather similar to an echo, and I realized the source must be underground and probably issued from the cellars.

Not wanting to risk being seen I hurried back to the bedroom. Once, glancing down the short flight of stairs I was startled to see a pale round face staring upwards like the disc of a watery moon through cloud.

Jed.

So after all he *had* been about.

I stopped for a second, and put a finger to my lips in a

gesture of caution. The head nodded. 'Sh-sh,' I whispered or rather hissed, 'you and me, Jed. A secret; just you and me.' I doubted if he could properly hear, my voice was too low. But the nod became wilder, so I knew he understood.

My heart was beating heavily against my eardrums when I reached the room – I didn't think he'd ever harm me, but instinct told me you could never be sure with half-wits, and if his mood changed? I shivered, and just to be on the safe side turned the key in the lock. Then I crossed to the side window. The view from there was completely in shade. Only a single light twinkled occasionally from the misted cliff.

To ease apprehension I went to the small table where a plate of sandwiches waited, probably left by Joel on Justin's instructions, and poured a cup of milk from the jug. There was also a small glass of wine; but I didn't drink that, wanting to keep my head clear. By then I was too restless to feel hungry, but ate a little and drank the milk. The light by that time was very bad. I looked for my candle but there was none; usually I took one myself from the kitchen when I went to bed. Irritation enlivened me. Really! I thought Justin might at least have seen that I wasn't left in darkness. But of course it was all part of the plan to keep me out of things.

How long would it be, I wondered, before something happened.

I was changing my mind and about to take a sip of the wine when the muffled thudding I'd heard previously recommenced. Hooves? Only nearer this time. I listened intently, then went to the small lookout of a window, peering into the dark grey of evening fog. Once more I saw a light flash from somewhere inland near the cliff. I was aware of things happening, although it was impossible to decipher any concrete shape or form. But as my eyes grew more accustomed to the darkness I fancied darker shapes moving, humped close and furtively, to bushes and rocks above the sea, and the blurred shadowed forms of small boats astir on the water.

There was an accentuation of sound for a brief few seconds. It seemed the floor of the room shook, then suddenly quietened, and I told myself that what I'd heard could have been a distortion, intensified, of some natural phenomenon from underground. Then I recalled the dark tunnel to the cellars, the labyrinth of passages and the eerie cave containing the wealth of treasures and the woman's portrait, and knew there must be some connection and that I was on the brink of some wild adventure.

I had not undressed that night, and was about to reach for my cape when a shot shattered the silence followed by a volley of gunfire.

Unheeding of Justin's instructions I ran from the room and raced down the stairs to the kitchen. Joel was standing in the glow of the fire stirring something in a large black cooking pot. He drew up and faced me belligerently as I burst in. I noticed everything else was in comparative darkness; shutters were down over the windows as though to exclude all contact with outside.

'What you doin' here?' he said, 'you edn' no right to be paradin' about this time o' night. I've Master Justin's orders, missus. There's things happenin' out there – things not fit f'r any wumman. So you just get back to where you come from. An' no trouble, see?'

I realized there was no point in arguing with him. I'd be no match for him in any physical struggle and knew he felt his first obligation would always be in a fanatical duty to Justin. Apart from that the smell of cooking tempted me. I was already shivering from nerves and chill.

'I won't give you any trouble,' I answered, 'but I've not had much to eat today, and that broth – it *is* broth, isn't it, Joel? – smells so good.' I paused, fancying his expression had relaxed slightly, then continued, 'I don't think my – Mr Justin would mind me having a taste, would he?' I smiled pleadingly, and apparently he was disarmed.

'Very well,' he agreed grudgingly, 'but you just sit there, on that stool, missus, where I c'n kep'n eye on you. There's no trustin' wummen – no way't all.'

'But I'm supposed to be a *boy*, Joel,' I pointed out.

A faint quirk of humour tilted one shaggy eyebrow – the first I'd ever seen on his grim countenance.

'Doan' you try'n charm *me*,' he remarked, wagging a ladle at me. 'I've not lived sixty-five years without learning to know a female when I sees one. *Or* her wily ways, an' that's f'r sure.'

'Oh, I realize that,' I answered demurely.

'Hm. Well, then.' He poured two large ladlesful of broth into a bowl and handed it to me. I took it gratefully and at the same moment a further volley of shots sounded from outside followed by a tumult of shouting and thud of galloping horses' hooves.

I tried to visualize something of what was going on, and wondered if Captain Fitzgerald was involved, and in what way Justin was concerned. Suddenly dread and fear for him swamped every other emotion in me. My appetite died. I'd already swallowed much of the broth, but couldn't finish it. I pushed the bowl away and got up. Joel started to remonstrate. I shook my head. 'Don't worry, I'm staying here. But – they're smuggling, aren't they, Joel?' I asked desperately. 'Mr Justin? He's part of it? That's true, isn't it? *Isn't* it?'

He shook his head as though facing an impossible issue. For once his feelings showed; he looked different – human.

'You doan' know half of et,' he said slowly. 'There's more to et than that, much, much more. An' doan' you go thinkin' bad o' my master. Seen him through many a battle I have, an' a braver man never walked the earth nor sailed the seas than him.'

'I'm sure. But—'

My words were broken by an escalation of sound including male voices yelling over the moor somewhere above, but nearby the house. Joel stood with grizzled head raised listening, still as a statue, staring at the door.

Gradually the wild crescendo faded until it was submerged by only intermittent creakings and reverberations of the night's happenings.

For a few minutes there was complete motionless silence between the old man and myself. Then he brushed me aside and was moving to go out, when the door broke open and Justin staggered in. He had a gun in one hand, the other arm hung loosely at his side. A thin pale moon had risen outside streaking across the floor, lighting the drops of blood dripping from his coat sleeve across the flagstones. His face was a ghastly grey. I reached forward but he waved me aside and cried thickly, 'Give me a drink.'

Joel already had a flask ready and a bench drawn to what remained of the fire.

'Here y'are master. Sit down. What've those devil's spawn done t'you—'

Justin flung himself down, looking up, and forced a grin. 'It's what I've done to them, Joel. Those devils are gone now – for many a year to come, let's hope.'

He suddenly seemed to be aware of me. His voice was wry when he said, 'And so, Kim, this is your first glimpse of a man's world, I'll be bound. Hope you're enjoying it. Blood and thunder, eh?'

Knowing he was play-acting and in pain, I ignored his tone.

'You're hurt,' I said as calmly as possible. 'You should take your coat off and let me look at the arm. If it's bad we should get a doctor, or—'

'*Doctor*? Oh? So now we have a little *nurse* in boy's clothing.'

I flinched. 'I'm serious. *Please.*'

He frowned, wincing at the same time, and dropped the acting. 'I told you not to interfere. And get this into your head. I'm having no doctor or stranger fussing about me. What I have's a mere scratch.'

'Scratches can be dangerous, and you're bleeding badly. Look at the floor.'

'Then get me a towel instead of talk, talk – *talk*.'

He leaned back.

'I'll do that,' I heard Joel saying, 'an' a bowl of water.' He crossed to the sink, but Justin, to my great surprise, said, 'I can tend myself. Let the girl do any fetching and carrying. It's a woman's work, what she's here for. You can go off now, Joel. Take a bit of bed now you've got the chance. There'll be a few plunderers about, and an eye on the stable's necessary. No local's going to track any horse of mine with you around. Keep your lamp burning and gun ready. That's all.'

I knew Joel had his own sleeping-quarters in the loft above the stables, and was a good shot. Once or twice he'd come into the kitchen holding a dead rabbit dangling from a hand. I'd winced inwardly, disliking him for shooting the innocent creature. But then perhaps that was part of the man's life that Justin referred to.

I wondered, as Justin dismissed him, if he could as easily kill any man who endangered his master's safety, and from the brief hostility for me on the hard old face, I decided he could – easily.

When Joel had left, Justin faced me from under lowered brows. His expression was dark. 'I thought I told you to keep out of the way,' he remarked.

'And so I did, while that shooting went on,' I answered defiantly. 'But you need me now, don't you?'

'What the devil do you mean – *need* you? I need no woman. You can wipe that mess up off the floor and fetch me a damn cloth. That's all I need.'

'Oh, Justin,' I broke in, 'whether woman or man, you need more than just a cloth. And you owe me the right to tend you. I've play-acted the wife for you, and stood your bullying, let you cut my hair and pretended to be a boy, and all for what? – just to learn that my great uncle's dead, yet not another word about when, or where he lies. Is that fair? You know it isn't.'

For a moment or two he seemed to forget his pain. His

eyebrows arched, and it seemed to me there was a whimsical tilt to his mouth.

He made some sardonic remark but I ignored it, suggesting that unless he was prepared to bleed to death he should extricate his arm from his jacket himself or allow me to do it for him.

'There's such a thing as blood poisoning,' I remarked.

'What do you know about that? Were you a nurse?'

'Of my mother,' I told him, 'for quite a time. We had a difficult life.'

'Hm. 'Tis all coming back to you then?'

'Not quite all. But that – yes. Oh, *please* Justin. Do let me be of some use now.'

He agreed grudgingly; the pain as I helped remove the thick material from the torn flesh must have been intense, and there were moments when I felt almost sick myself. But at last the wound was washed and bound with towelling from a cupboard.

'Perhaps you should have a sling,' I suggested.

'A *sling*? For this?' He got to his feet. 'It's only superficial. Is *that* what you're after? To have me like some puny invalid under your command? Forget it, and go now where you belong. To your bed.'

'*No*,' I said, 'I won't. I've told you – I've been bullied and ordered about enough.' I was shaking inwardly, but I faced him squarely, both fists clenched at my side. I watched something flutter in his face I'd not seen there before – something holding an unknowable challenge that also stimulated the fiercely developing bond between us.

'So you will not?' he said, taking a step towards me.

'I've said.'

Before I was hardly aware of it, his good arm was round my waist, and I was being pressed to his firm body so hard and close I could hardly breathe.

'But I think you will,' he said. 'I'm still capable of dragging any rebellious female by the hair of her head to her rightful place if I've a mind to. And by Gad I've a mind to, my darling. Do you hear? Do you understand, Isabella? This night, though it's only for an hour maybe, we'll lie together.'

And that is how it was. The kitchen was left in disarray, everything forgotten but the wild hunger of belonging. I went blindly where Justin willed, swept on a thrilling tide of rapture to a culmination beyond time or reason, and he was everywhere round me and in me, flesh to flesh, every pulse between us throbbing in wild delight. For the first time I knew myself both soul and body as a woman – Justin's woman. And when the final moment came it was as though the whole world flowered in a blinding fountain of ecstasy. Then, gradually came quietness – velvet soft, holding the deep and after-peace of consummation.

When I woke I was alone. There was a deep indentation in the bed where his body had lain, and the oak bedposts had a rosy glow from the morning sun streaking through the curtains, turning the stains of blood on the quilt to a deeper red. Though at peace, my mind and body quivered in the sea of emotional release. I glanced round expecting to see the familiarity of Cook's room, but the surroundings were different. This bedroom was larger, more sumptuous, the ceiling high and encrusted, the hangings and furniture heavier and richer. There were no feminine fripperies about, and I knew as the memories crowded back, causing a warm blush to spread through my whole body, that it was a man's room – Justin's – where we'd spent those few night hours.

I found, to my embarrassment, but with no shame, that I was quite naked; but an embroidered silk wrap lay over the foot of the bed, obviously left there for me, because there was no sign of my boy's clothes.

Though still physically tired, I got up and slipped it on, recalling the evening's caresses – the sensuous stimulus of his hands over my skin thrilling my body's most secret places to life – running his fingers through my hair, and his lips hot and demanding travelling from neck to thighs while I yearned towards him.

This was love then, this deepest, most wonderful communication of intimacy possible between man and woman.

Spirit or flesh?

Both, both, *both* my heart cried. And it would be the same with him. It *must* be. It couldn't be otherwise. But I was wrong.

So terribly wrong. It wasn't like that at all.

When I went down to the kitchen in the morning he was there alone, without Joel, slumped by the dying fire and when he looked up I fancied he had not rested at all. There was no welcome in his haggard face, no gesture of a smile on his lips or faintest pleasure at seeing me. It was as though renewed shock had shattered any feeling there'd been between us. Only a wild and bitter condemnation.

'Jed's gone,' he said. 'Drowned. His body was swept up

on the tide – with the others. I've had it taken away.'

'Oh,' I remarked pointlessly. 'I'm sorry.'

'Spare the platitudes. He was a poor creature who should never have been born, but as he had been he'd a right to his life.' There was a short pause. 'Anyway, *you'll* be all right now. You're free to claim your inheritance and your treasures. Miss Isabella Teale, heiress to the late Jeremiah Teale of Carnwikken.'

I was at a loss, frozen with cold chilling disappointment, but managed to ask, 'What do you mean, Justin?'

His stern mouth took a sardonic, lopsided twist. 'You'll have a full explanation shortly, no doubt, when the law arrives. At the moment, I'm damned if I'm in a mood for talking. Just get yourself ready to return to your rightful abode. I'm sure you'll make a splendid mistress – with Silas and Susannah taken.'

'Taken?' I echoed. 'Where?'

'Bodmin,' he said abruptly. 'Gaol. The lock-up – for transportation, or worse – where and whenever the law decides fit. But that's not your affair, and don't fret me with any more questions. Just hold your tongue for a bit and leave me to straighten things up here.' Before I could speak he added wryly, 'Though if that ever will be possible Lord alone knows.'

I shivered, then stiffened with resentment, and a bitter sense of disillusionment.

'Why are you talking to me like this? I realize awful things have happened out there. But is there any reason to push me out – after – after last night?'

His glance at me was direct, unflinching and enigmatical, showing no feeling whatsoever.

'Last night has nothing to do with it, and shouldn't have happened. Today's reality, You're nothing to me, Isabella. A few moments out of time, that's all. And for God's sake, don't look so helpless and lost. You've got a life ahead. So get on with it. Pack your things – what you've got. Joel's waiting down there to see you in Carnwikken. Don't you *understand*?' His voice was hard, desperate.

'No. No, I don't.'

'Then let me spell it out for you: no woman in the world matters to me or ever will any more. I have my own work here at Falk and that's all I need.'

'And what about *me*? Don't I count with you a bit? There are things I can do for you. Or have you just *used* me? You always said everything would be all right, and you'd explain – *everything*. Yes, you did, Justin – about the war, and opium and how Silas and Susannah were concerned, and me being attacked – and the treasures in the case – the picture of the woman there – *everything* that went on when I couldn't remember—' The words broke from me in a rush of confusion and ended in a choke of threatened tears.

He turned on his heel. 'So I've broken my word. Good. 'Tis better you should know me as I really am – a disillusioned rake and rogue who takes a girl he fancies then leaves her to go to the devil. A buccaneer of the worst kind. With you it'd been a bit different. A few kisses between us, no more – until that last time – God knows why, you were always quite responsive. I suppose it was your innocence. Blackguard that I am, I was never one to take a woman at a disadvantage. Why worry? You have a fortune waiting, and no doubt some lusty young buck will soon appear ready to share it, together with your delightful body—'

'Stop it,' I interrupted. 'How *can* you? You must be drunk: I believe you are.'

He waved a hand in negation. The haggard lines of his face deepened with sardonic boredom.

'Have done, Isabella, you weary me. Get out of my sight, do. You should have heard enough by now.'

Dumbly I watched him go to the door which he opened before putting his hand to his mouth and calling, 'Joel, Mistress Teale will be with you in two shakes of a lamb's tail.'

I still didn't move.

He looked back once before leaving.

'Farewell. It's been an education meeting you.' He gave a mock bow, and the farce was over. The latch closed and with it my resistance died. The tears that had been gathering steadily to my eyes fell slowly down my cheeks.

I was crying.

Farewell was such a dreadful word; but he'd meant it, and I wondered how I'd bear it.

The walk over the moor to Carnwikken was a desolate experience holding once again the unreal atmosphere of a dream – a dead nightmarish dream. Beside me the figure of Joel strode silently, head hunched against the wind, his black-tailed coat flapping like the wings of some monstrous crow. Below on my right, pieces of flotsam from the night's malpractice lay dark against the pale sands. The skeleton of a large four-masted boat struck sharp under the leaden grey sky. A few figures poked among the rocks and debris. Gulls shrieked through the thin air and I thought I still smelled the lingering pungent tang of gunfire.

I thought of Jed's body and those others referred to by Justin taken to destruction by the tide, and shuddered. As the shape of the house with the gargoyles drew near I had an almost overbearing impulse to rush away – somewhere, *anywhere* where life was normal and people ordinary decent human beings. But where could I run to?

At a certain point we cut down the slope of land and arrived at the gate of the court where I'd been taken by Mistress Susannah. The thought of her, the frightening image, returned with a shock. But, of course, she wouldn't be there now, if, as Justin had said, she'd been taken by the law; and he would have had no reason to lie.

A man in uniform, wearing a tricorn black hat, scarlet coat, cream breeches, and black boots, was posted in the entry. It is curious why and how I noticed such details. But the scene remains imprinted on my mind as though etched on the elements – the grey granite walls against the cold sky relieved only by that one splash of colour. He stepped aside as we approached, indicating the door that was half open. I went through, thinking Joel would follow, but he didn't. He muttered something under his breath and turned back, leaving me to make my own way into the house.

I hadn't far to go before reaching the kitchens.

Two soldiers were idling before a roasting fire. One jumped to attention when I appeared, and motioned me through to the main hall which I recalled quite clearly, then to the library near the garden room where I'd been presented to Captain Fitzgerald.

He was there, in his officer's uniform this time, looking somewhat out of place against the scholarly interior of books.

'Ah! Miss Teale,' he said, coming towards me with his arms outspread. 'At last I can be allowed to greet you in your proper status under your rightful name, and as *myself*.'

I felt his warm hands close on mine, and knew indeed it was him.

'Captain Fitzgerald,' I said feebly, going to meet him.

'That is so. And a thousand apologies for the former subterfuge. But—' he paused, before adding, 'It was, I'm afraid, quite necessary at the time.'

'Oh?' I couldn't say 'I see' because I didn't.

'Yes. Now do come and sit down. You must be cold after that walk over the moor.'

'Not because of the walk,' I told him, 'but the circumstances. They are so very strange, sir.'

'Yes, yes, of course. And we shall need a little time to discuss matters, if only briefly. So please—'

He indicated a bench in an alcove where logs glowed invitingly from a deeply set grate in an elaborately carved fireplace. I sat, and he took a place opposite to me.

'As I've already said – a monstrous trick had to be played on you at our first meeting,' he remarked, with a tentative half smile. 'For that again I apologize, but it was necessary for your own sake, and as proof to me of your identity and the circumstances of your presence at Carnwikken.'

'Oh?' I waited.

'Yes, indeed. Luckily the plan worked. You must agree,

Miss Teale, that the shock of hearing the name
Carnwikken jerked your memory to life, giving your
identity not only to you but to me and others concerned in
the dramatic and sorry story.'

'I shall be grateful to hear the explanation,' I said primly.
'I've had a difficult and rather terrible time lately. Will you
be acting for the police?'

'My work is concerned with the Preventative – as well
as police and military matters.' There was a short pause
before he added, 'But I'm sure my personal status is of
secondary importance at this moment. First of all comes
your peace of mind and satisfaction that all is being done
now to make amends on your behalf. There'll be no more
tricks, I can assure you.'

'Thank you.'

He got up suddenly, walked to one of the long windows
facing the moors, stood with his hands behind his back
staring out reflectively, then turned and came back.

'You must be aware now that Mr Llarne has been
helping us over the nasty business involving the attack on
you and your subsequent confinement here, which until a
month or two ago was your late uncle – Jeremiah Teale's
home?'

I nodded. 'I suppose so.'

'A strange man and an adventurous one. He'd been
involved with the Trevanions for a considerable time in
unsavoury matters concerning smuggling; on the other
hand, without his help you certainly wouldn't be in the
position of talking to me now. In fact you mightn't even be
alive at all.'

My heart gave an unnerving jerk. 'You mean—?'

'I mean you could be dead. If there were ever a more black-hearted couple of criminals than those two it's doubtful. *Now.*' His voice deepened before he added, 'This is not the time for a full explanation. You will have that from the lawyers later. But briefly, for some months before your uncle's death, the sly pair had been robbing him cunningly – not only by drawing their weekly salary and sum for household expenditure under a forged signature, but by deviously secreting his treasures – Jeremiah was a collector of valuable antique pieces – in the tunnel under Falk – to be shipped on a certain date with a load of smuggled opium originally from India. The war with China was already on. France was involved, with Britain, which made shipping a comparatively simple business. The date of the boat's arrival was set provisionally and the Trevanions' departure with their spoils arranged. After delivery and payment for the drugs, Silas and Susannah would sail for Ireland, I believe, and then where, God knows. But they were a canny pair, all seemed possible until *you* arrived.'

'Oh.'

'They'd had a letter from you, of course, informing your uncle of your arrival, but he'd been dead for some time though no one knew it. So you had to be silenced. Either kidnapped or murdered. The first seemed safest. With you drugged and incapable some story could be woven concerning your presence at Carnwikken – if by any unlikely chance it was discovered. But *murder!* – well, even a knave like Silas might hesitate. So—' He broke off. A number of unanswered questions left the story a mystery, including how and why Justin had been concerned.

As if seeing the unspoken query Captain Fitzgerald said, 'Justin Llarne's permission had to be given for use of his coastal territory for smuggling purposes. As I've already said, he's a colourful, strange character with no conscience concerning certain aspects of contraband activity – brandy, perhaps, lace, silks – but over the opium plot *no*. He'd consented for some reason of his own to play the part of your husband – perhaps as a dominant factor in keeping you there, believing the Trevanions' story at first, anyway, that you'd fallen and were suffering acute shock and loss of memory. Now when he noticed you were drugged and learned that the true contents of the expected cargo included opium – he came clean with the Revenue and police, consequently we were ready for the brig when it arrived.'

'But *why* had I to be Mrs Llarne?'

'In case you were seen by chance by an unexpected caller at Carnwikken, and to install a sense of his power into you. He's a very dominant personality.'

'But I could just as well have been Susannah's niece – or relative of some sort. Better.'

'Oh, no. As Justin's woman – and by villagers he was regarded as an eccentric having his own secret relationships – you were embroiled more in their scheme – so long as you were drugged and incapable of rationally denying it. And remember he was being blackmailed. It was important for him to appear to go along with them. Silas had threatened to inform against him otherwise, concerning the shooting and murder of the Revenue man. His evidence would have been extremely condemning.'

'But that wasn't true.'

'No. But Silas was such a wily creature and murder's a capital offence. Another thing' – he paused and after a slight smile resumed – 'hasn't it occurred to you that Llarne himself might have relished the idea?'

I flushed. 'No. I – he – he always seemed against any *idea* of marriage with anyone.'

'Well, I advise you to look at things from another angle now. Human beings can be very unpredictable, Miss Teale, and if I may say so without offence, you are an extremely attractive young woman. So let us leave the pros and cons and forget complexities, shall we? Now ...' he gave me a very hard stare, 'by rights maybe I'm saying more than I should at this stage, the courts will be the final assessors of this ugly business. But all *you* will have to do is to prove your identity, which should be simple, with Justin Llarne's backing, and my own, of course. In the meantime I suggest you move for a while to the village while things are settled and put into order here. I believe you are old Jeremiah's only inheritor. That will easily be proved. In the meantime I can arrange for a lawyer from Truro to see you. There's a pleasant coach house in the village, the Goat and Flag, run by a decent elderly couple, the Baragwanaths, Tom and his wife Ellen. Comfortable and good food, as I've discovered myself.'

His voice began to sound mechanically in my ears. I felt dazed, but one thought remained uppermost.

My uncle.

'You say my uncle's dead. Mr – Mr Llarne said so too. Will you – shall I be able to see where he's buried?'

'My dear young lady, of course. But no doubt he will be given an official burial later when the law is satisfied all is in order. At the moment try and think of the future, happier things than the dead and what is past.' He smiled, and I felt heartened, following Justin's rebuff.

Little more was discussed before I set off with the captain for The Goat and Flag. The light had lifted a little, and as we approached the high rim of the moor the tips of rooftops and chimneys appeared clear against the grey sky. The air freshened, holding the tang of bracken and gorse mingled with the salty drift of brine drawn from the sea below. We walked sharply and were soon at the village which was little more than a hamlet, huddled in a slight dip of the hill. Grey stone cottages crouched around a grassy square, with a squat church on one side and the inn on the other, facing it. A signboard depicting a goat waving a flag creaked in a rising wind. The hostelry was low-roofed, probably Elizabethan, with a four-pillared porch on a low roof. I found the proprietor and his wife pleasant country folk, as Captain Fitzgerald had predicted, sociable but with something withheld and a little secretive about them that was a characteristic I discovered later of the Cornish people.

The room I was allotted was pleasantly furnished, with a large oak bedstead covered by a patchwork quilt, a washstand and dressing-table, and a round pedestal table near the window. There was a spindle-backed chair nearby, a chest with a Bible on it, and hanging on a wall an oleograph of the Battle of Trafalgar.

A faint smell of lavender managed to penetrate the overhanging scent of malt and liquor. Lace curtains drifted faintly in the draught from the window, looking as though they were newly washed, between heavy crimson drapes on either side.

'You can have those drawn at night or if you do feel chilled,' my landlady said a trifle smugly. 'The best bedroom this is, and all we do wish is to know our guests are comfortable. So if there's anything particular you fancy that isn't provided you're only to say, and the same for food. Jenny, our girl, is a good hand at cooking and will do her best for thee.'

I thanked her, and when she'd gone took the things I'd brought out of the valise, realizing how few they were and wondering what could be done about necessary washing.

However, that was a problem that would have to wait for a few days. My first priority was to get matters settled with the lawyer, whom Captain Fitzgerald had told me before he left was due to visit me at the inn the next day.

Despite the comfort of my new surroundings, it was hours before sleep came that night. My mind was a whirl with restless conjecturing concerning past events and picturing the future. It seemed incredible that after the terrifying period of uncertainty when I'd been virtually a prisoner in the callous care of the ruthless Trevanions, I was to be declared mistress of the very premises of my torment, my own home that had belonged to Jeremiah Teale, my great uncle.

But yet it was so.

The lawyer – a sober-looking portly gentleman, in black clothes wearing a long-tailed coat and stove hat, and carrying a case of documents, arrived in the afternoon. We met in the bar parlour, which had been given a special spit-and-polish earlier and a bottle of the landlord's best port put ready, with glasses on a side table.

During the hour he was with me I proved to his satisfaction that I was indeed Isabella Teale and in a daze I signed documents and learned that when the necessary court procedures were finalized I should be quite a rich woman. 'Mr Teale had not only inherited a fortune through family,' he said somewhat portentously, 'he had been a collector of fine arts and treasures for a considerable part of his life. These will no doubt have to be valued, but I can assure you, my dear young lady, in the meantime, while any necessary legal enquiries are undertaken, I am in the happy position of being able to deposit a very comfortable sum of money under your name in a bank for your benefit.' He paused, then added, 'I do not suppose you have any particular choice of where, or *which* bank?'

'No,' I told him, feeling quite bewildered by a confusion of emotions. 'I'd rather you did all that for me. I don't know anything about such things.' After the difficult circumstances of my childhood it would certainly be a relief and exciting to have money to spend on myself without worry, although underlying everything was the hurt of Justin Llarne's rejection and, of course, my uncle's death.

I hoped to learn something that would give a clue as to why Justin had behaved so cruelly following our brief passion, but though I tried once or twice to guide the lawyer's mind in this direction, he refused to show any interest, and guided the subject to that of the Opium War, the activities of the East India Company, the alliance of Britain with France against the Chinese – and evils of the deadly drug which was being smuggled into this country.

When I queried stubbornly in what way the Trevanions had been concerned, he refused to make direct comment, being far less informative than Justin had been. Indeed, except for hearing of any financial benefits I learned very little at all. Lawyers, I supposed, had to be ambiguous over certain affairs, I realized when he'd left, and it meant a great deal knowing how my future would be taken care of. The addresses of furnishers, and a builder had been given to me, and I'd been assured Pollyvers and Congay, Solicitors, would be in constant communication with me and at hand when I needed advice.

Oh, yes; a good deal of excitement lay ahead.

But loneliness too. Loneliness that was a kind of agony without Justin. In spite of my determination to sweep him from my thoughts, I couldn't, and in the bitter moments when I recollected those brief hours together, I almost hated him for what he'd been, and done to me.

During the next few days, in leisure moments from business matters concerning my newly acquired estate and journeys to Truro for shopping, I would retrace my steps over the moor to a spot overlooking Falk. Sometimes in the distance I'd see Justin in a small boat setting out for fishing, I presumed; only a dot on the expanse of water, but recognizable in the sunlight – and in a flash of anger I determined to win him back or make him suffer.

But how? He was a man of his word, and I had no intention of being humiliated again.

'You do know the gentleman, Master of Falk, do you?' my landlady queried one day when I returned to The Goat and Flag.

'Slightly,' I told her, guessing from the certain quick, almost sly glance of her small eyes that she'd heard stories of intriguing happenings from village folk. And what she didn't know she might have made up. My wanderings Falk way had obviously been noticed and all local folk must all have been aware of the drug raid by the Preventative, of the Trevanions being taken off to Bodmin, and Jed's death. Also that of my uncle.

'A sad story, that of Jed,' she remarked on another occasion – it was raining, and the rain merged sea and sky into one like a grey shroud driven on the wind. 'A poor sick thing he was, but begotten like he was what could you expect?'

When I made no comment she went on, 'Incest o' course.'

'Incest?'

'That's what they do say. Born to Susannah by her brother.'

'Oh.' A feeling of nausea seized me. 'I didn't know.'

'Well, you wouldn't, my dear, would you? And it was never spoken of, because that unpleasant creature Silas was such a one for praying and judging folk and making out he was holier than all the rest.' She drew a deep breath and continued, 'How old Master Teale could've ever trusted him in the first place – and he managed his affairs, Silas did, for all of nine years – I do not know. But there! Your poor uncle's been out of it for quite a time now, I do hear. Must be more'n a month gone, according to what they say, and all that time there was those two collecting expenses for theirselves, pretending Master Teale was well on the way to recovery from his illness, milking him dry. At least doin' their best to. But I understand you've been left very comfortable, my dear?'

Finding her questioning becoming rather unpleasant, I diverted the conversation by saying, 'My financial affairs aren't settled yet, so I don't know. My business at the moment is to get Carnwikken into order. There's quite a lot to be done; but the solicitors have arranged for builders to visit the house as soon as possible, and a valuer too, I think. It'll all take time.'

'Yes. O' course. Well, I hope your stay's a happy one here. And don't go listening to gossip. Things've always been said about that old gentleman – your uncle living above there.'

'My *great* uncle,' I corrected her.

She looked mildly taken aback. 'Oh, yes. I forgot. There's a generation or two between you. Or *was* – until the old man was taken. But he was a rare character. *Collected* things, they say. Rare stuff worth a load.'

I nodded, saying nothing more on the subject but remembering the heap of precious articles stored in the rambling cellars of Falk. And the portrait of the woman. Had that too once belonged to Great Uncle Jeremiah? I didn't think so, recalling Justin's reaction when I'd referred to it in the past. I knew it had meant something intensely personal to him, and the knowledge hurt.

Just as quickly as the dreary weather had fallen over the district, the sky lifted suddenly and pale sunlight flooded the landscape and sea.

On a clear afternoon I decided in a wave of impulse to take a walk over the moors and cut down to the rugged beach of caves and inlets surrounding Falk.

There was a short cut from the village leading past the opposite side of the house of the chimney which I judged couldn't be more than two miles or so; I hadn't tried it before in case of bumping into Justin unexpectedly. But now I didn't care if I did. To the contrary, the thought of any contact at all, however embarrassing, was far preferable to having none, and excitement grew in me as I clambered down the steepening path between gorse and undergrowth.

Everywhere was very calm when I reached the pale strip of sand bordering the inlet. On my right the coast stretched as a kind of estuary changing on the far side from rocky cliffs to sandy dunes alternating with the granite. A thread of road wound ribbon-like from the coast to the moorland hills in the far distance, and along there I imagined the horsemen of the Revenue had probably ridden on the night of their attack. I paused reflectively for some minutes, realizing once more how very little I really knew about the wild events of that fateful night, how secretive even the Baragwanaths had been concerning the actual affairs, and the villagers completely uncommunicative. Yet I'd seen for myself from the distance dots of figures moving about the beach and had heard that the son of the postmistress had been killed in 'an accident'. I'd watched from the inn the dismal little procession of the funeral cortège passing to the church.

There was Jed too. And Willy Portreath, a fisherman. And others? Yes, there must have been other victims during a night of such savagery. Yet a veil of stubborn secrecy persisted.

'The less you know of it,' Mrs Baragwanath had said,

'the better for you and f'r all of us. You've enough to think about, getting that big house right for living in without bothering 'bout any nasty business. You should've had enough with Silas and his sister. Leave Cornish affairs to those whose business it is. That's my advice.'

And with that I'd had to be satisfied.

But an air of mystery and almost festering isolation clogged the atmosphere on that particular day of my ramble. As I passed the upper gate of the house, I steeled my senses for any sound or sight of human habitation. But there was none. Although I'd half feared an encounter with Justin, I'd wildly hoped for it – anything to break the rift between us. But there was no sign of him – only his small boat lying idly on the rim of the calm tide. The wall of Falk rose high above, almost as bleak and dark as the cliffs sharp against the clear sky which predicted rain, I supposed, later.

I made my way past crevices and jutting crags, skirting small pools where sodden relics of the night's plunder lay as sordid reminders of the cruel happenings. In a wave of revived terror I recalled Jed, and wondered where he now lay. In the churchyard? Or some distant mortuary? The memory of him and his death made me realize with a feeling of shock that I could never really like Carnwikken. The atmosphere would be too tainted with frightening recollections of the past. I would stay for a bit perhaps, until it was put in proper order and then sell it. After that? I just couldn't visualize the future at all.

The sky suddenly darkened as a grey cloud dimmed the fitful sun. Rounding a jutting corner I found myself facing the stretch of beach where the tunnel led from its hole to the cellars of Falk.

I paused at the entrance, with my heart pumping, seized by an intangible fear. What should I find there? The momentary stab of terror was not of Justin; I knew, however unpleasant he might be, he would never harm me. But still, yes, I sensed that something unpredictable threatened me from within. The impulse seized me to hurry past and either go forward to Carnwikken, or turn back and retrace my footsteps the way I'd come.

Then I changed my mind, and plunged into the dark passage of menacing stillness.

The cold icy smell of weed and dripping walls hung in the air like a shroud. I went on; there was no sign of movement or life at all, nothing but the splash, splash of moisture, and the hollow swish of my own footsteps through the dampness. A moist cobweb or swinging filament of weed from above caught my forehead as I approached the curve leading to the spreading space where the treasures had been. I went on, impelled by irrational curiosity, following the thin beam of light ahead.

Then I was there.

But the assortment of precious relics and articles had gone.

Only the portrait remained of the collection, lying slashed and torn in a stain of darkness that could have been paint or – blood. I stood still staring for a moment, shocked by this evidence of vandalism, although there must have been far worse, of a human kind, during the recent terrible events.

This after all was only a portrait.

Yet as I stood staring, the eyes seemed to burn with

curious life, holding contempt with it. Or sardonic amusement at my astonishment. Heaped behind it were a number of immense bags and boxes. Clothes, too – feminine garments that must once have been beautiful but were now a tangle of muddled silks and torn frippery, most of it roped into a bundle fit only for the dust-cart. A few ribbons and laces lay like forbidden sea creatures over the muddied floor.

Perhaps I gave an exclamation; I don't know, but suddenly I became aware of something else. I had the strongest sensation of being watched, and peering intently beyond the mass of rubble saw a figure. It had a familiarity about the stance and contour that was unmistakable – Justin. For a second or two we didn't move, just stood confronting each other until he stepped towards me. His head was slightly thrust forward; despite the fitful light I could see he was frowning.

I didn't move or draw back.

'What are you doing here?' he asked harshly. 'Back again so soon. Curiosity? But I thought I'd made it clear you weren't wanted. It's a sad state when a man can't be free of some wilful minx's attentions for a few moments of his life.'

'I'm sorry. I—'

'No, you're not. You're not sorry at all; you're just a damned nuisance. In the past I promised you a sound walloping to teach you a bit of sense. Maybe this is the moment.'

He stood very close to me. I didn't flinch. It was impossible to see his expression then, but I managed to say with a confidence I didn't feel, 'That's up to you.'

There was a pause. He turned away abruptly, kicked a pile of rubble, then faced me again with yards between us, and this time the wan light shone on his face briefly, accentuating haggard lines of strain and tiredness.

'That's right,' he said, 'it's up to me, and I don't choose. There's no urge in me for that sort of thing now. If you must know, I was about to perform a funeral service – the funeral of my past. Now it will have to wait for the next high tide when the waves can carry it away.'

'Funeral service?' I echoed bleakly.

'That's so, madam,' he said, indicating the assortment of bags and boxes, 'because *you* with the devilish knack you have of appearing at the wrong moment have delayed the sordid little scene.'

'Oh, but I needn't,' I cried impetuously, 'I'll go this very moment and leave you to your—'

'Celebration?' he interrupted mockingly. 'But you certainly will not. Tiresome as it may be the remaining shred of gentlemanliness in me forbids allowing an important young woman to make her long trek back over the cliffs alone. I shall accompany you. We will stop for refreshment at Falk. And maybe – just *maybe* we can have a little civilized talk together. Do you think that's possible?'

'I don't know,' I answered honestly.

'Neither do I. Nevertheless we'll have a try.'

And so it was that contrary to all expectations Justin Llarne and I set off together for the house with the chimneys.

7

I'd had moments of resentment on the way to Falk for allowing Justin to accompany me following his belligerence and angry verbal attack in the cave. But then I could hardly have refused without creating a scene which could have resulted only in further humiliation. So I'd kept up as dignified a silence as I could muster, and when at last we reached the house my temper had eased into curiosity. What in the world had we to talk about any more? Just one question still rankled in my mind.

Why ever had he pretended to be my husband? I'd had Captain Fitzgerald's explanation, but surely there must be more to it than that?

I decided to say nothing until he spoke first. And when we – or rather I – was seated by the library fire, I became aware of a hesitant restlessness in him – a certain expectant watchfulness – which told me he was impatient for me to begin with my usual volley of questioning.

I waited.

He strode to a cupboard in a recess, and brought glasses and a decanter to a table. He was dressed in everyday clothes for out-of-doors, but the simplicity only emphasized his manliness, and when the light from the tall Gothic window caught the firm lines of his features, he looked incredibly handsome. My heart gave a little lurch. If only he really cared for me, I thought. But there was no emotion on his face, no touch of warmth.

'You'll have a brandy?' he said emotionlessly.

'I'm not used to spirits,' I said, and indeed this was true. In the memories I now had of my youth there'd been no money for liquor. I'd been brought up without a father – he'd died when I was a tiny child, leaving nothing but debts, and my mother had made a living as a part-time governess.

'There's always a first time,' Justin said. He poured two glasses and brought one across to me. At first I shook my head.

'I really don't—'

'Drink it,' he said, in his usual assertive way.

I made a pretence of doing so, taking just a sip.

Unexpectedly he gave a little smile. 'At that rate it will take quite a time to get you drunk, Isabella, or should I say Miss Teale?'

He's playing a part again, I thought, *acting*. And I wondered how he managed to display a change of moods so quickly and effectively with such apparent ease.

'I don't mind *what* you call me, Justin,' I replied, 'so long as—'

'So long as it's not Mrs Llarne.'

I knew then he was teasing, and felt affronted. He must realize how deeply he'd hurt me by his rejection. Or *did* he? Perhaps he'd never troubled to bother about what any woman felt, and was just content to enjoy one when he felt like it, as he'd said, and then conveniently push her aside and go his own way. I knew I ought not to bother about him at all. He had no place in my life; the way he'd shown me that had not only been wounding, but hateful. Yes, in a way I hated him now. But behind the hate excitement and a strange illogical longing still lingered. At all costs I meant somehow to win his respect.

So I managed to remark in steady tones, 'I think I've a right to know one thing – all the rest concerning you and me isn't important any more. *Why* did you try to make me believe I was your wife?'

He shrugged.

'No deep or devious reason, I can assure you. I wasn't after your fortune, if that's what you're wondering. It was Susannah's idea in the beginning. To have further authority over you in case you became difficult. I'm sure Fitzgerald explained the position up to a point. It was really necessary to have you as quiet and acquiescent as possible until they were safely out of the picture with their spoils, and she knew me to be – shall we say – a fairly dominant character with the devil of a fiery temper and a strong hand when necessary. With my backing the Trevanions' plan appeared to have no hitch.'

'So you went along with it?'

He shrugged again.

'Perhaps I was intrigued, too. It had its amusing side. My

senses were titillated, and as things happened you should thank your stars I *was* involved. My friend Fitzgerald has no doubt already pointed that out to you.'

'Yes, but—'

'Oh, have done with questions and dramatics. You think me a blackguard and a knave – a trickster of the worst calibre, a rake, a smuggler – so I am, all of them, and have been for some time. Ever since … but we'll leave it there, I've no fancy for remembering details of my sordid past, and by now I'm sure you've no wish to hear. But' – he gave me a long hard look, with all mockery and bravado gone. For a few seconds he looked vulnerable and years younger, and I had a wild and foolish longing to fly to him and press myself into his arms. Then I heard him saying, 'You should know this though, Isabella – I *knew nothing of that evil woman drugging you.* I believed her explanation of finding you unconscious from a fall and that your loss of memory was due to concussion. It was quite a time before the truth registered. And it was then I contacted the law.'

'I see.' I didn't know what else to say.

He coughed. 'So shall we put the past behind us now – *all* of it, the bad and the good and look to the future?'

My heart missed a beat, then raced on again, in hope until he continued, looking away, 'I have a proposition to make, a *business proposition.*'

Disappointed and bewildered, I echoed, '*Business* proposition? With me? What do you mean?'

'I've heard rumours that you may possibly be thinking of selling Carnwikken when everything is settled and the will proved. Of course this can only be idle talk at the moment, but if you do I'd like the chance of making the first offer.'

So cool, so calculated, so businesslike, and so unlike the unpredictable reckless character I'd grown used to.

I was astonished.

'I haven't decided anything yet,' I said, 'and in any case, you'd have to talk to my ... my solicitors. I don't see – it seems so strange – when you have Falk—'

'I *live* at Falk, it's my home. My reasons are my own, Isabella.'

His voice had become cold and stern. I felt again rebuffed, shut out from his life. I wondered in a recurring fit of misery if there was some other woman in the background – someone he wanted installed close to him. The idea suddenly put me on the defensive. 'I shall have to think about it. It would depend.'

'On what? The price? I have money to spare, quite sufficient I think to outbid anyone else interested. It's an old wreck of a place—'

'Not a wreck any more,' I interrupted, 'quite a bit's been done already, and the solicitors think it could fetch a good sum when repairs are finished. Really, Justin, I *do* think it's a strange time to get me to make decisions. It was my uncle's home, after all.'

'Your *great* uncle, as you've said before. Of course, if you intend to keep it as a monument to his sacred memory, that's your affair. Although your veneration could be misplaced. He was quite a character in his time – one of my own choice. A wicked old boy, but likeable. However,' he shrugged and continued, 'I'd go for the lot, and I wouldn't try to defraud you. His collection of valuables alone is worth a little fortune, and I'd pay the fair price of valuation. Of course, you know nothing of these, except the ones you saw at Falk. There were more in the Carnwikken vaults.'

'So it's those you *really* want?' I said.

'I want everything with the property. Anyway, I'm not going to waste any more words now. You're not in the mood, and I've other things to do than argue with a wilful woman. Think about it; and drink up that brandy. You look as if you still need it.'

I felt tired and subdued suddenly; he was probably right. The shred of scarf I'd worn over my head had fallen away, and strands of hair straggled over my forehead. I did as he said, and took the drink. Then I stood up. 'I think we should be going.' There was no pleasure to be looking untidy and plain before him. 'I must look a sight,' I added automatically.

To my surprise he smiled, and it was a nice smile, genuine. 'You could never look a sight, Isabella,' he told me. Something warm, gentler in his voice gave me sudden irrational hope.

'Justin, I—'

Just as quickly as he'd softened, he became impersonal again. 'Come along then,' he agreed. 'We'll have to go by the road. Can you ride? It's too much of a pull up the steep cliff path.'

'A horse, do you mean? No.'

'Then you can have your first lesson.'

So it was that Justin brought his own mare, Jet, from the stables, and minutes later he was leading her by the bridle with me seated in the saddle for the rest of the journey back to the Goat and Flag.

During my stay at the inn I looked in at Carnwikken frequently to see how things were progressing. The roof had had to be mended, dry rot in floors was being dealt with. There were still repairs to be done about the wall on the sea side which had suffered from certain erosions of land, and battering of the granite by the elements at one corner. A mason pointed out to me that a chunk of stone had crumbled from the nose of one of the gargoyles at the front of the house. Did I wish this to be mended? 'No,' I told him, 'a chip off the nose makes no difference. He's ugly anyway.'

So they remained as they'd always been, macabre guardians of the past and Uncle Jeremiah Teale's secrets, in defiance of the years and elements.

Occasionally I caught sight of Justin in the distance, and once I saw him cutting towards the lane leading to Falk, from the direction of the Goat and Flag. He didn't see me, but when I returned to the inn I was told by the landlord that he'd enquired if I was about, and after hearing I was probably at Carnwikken doing something or other there he'd ridden away in the direction of Falk.

'Did he leave a message?' I enquired.

'No, nothing except it didn't matter. He'd see you some other time probably.'

Yes, I'd thought, just to know if I'd decided to sell him the house.

Well, I hadn't. Not definitely, although whenever I was in the place alone, which was generally evenings after a walk before my evening meal, I was filled with an insidious sense of oppression, and knew that I myself could never live there. It was not only the shadowed corridors and deserted lofty rooms, the hollow lonely sounds of my own footsteps, or even the evil memories when I'd lived like a prisoner under the dark influence of the Trevanions, but a haunting loneliness that had its own identity.

Was I fretting still about Justin? Yes, I suppose deep down I was. But the longing for him had become hard and taut like a buried sword ready to defend any softening towards him. He had humiliated and rejected me.

Let him wait.

Mrs Baragwanath was curious. She had seen my return journey to the inn on Justin's horse, of course, and no doubt gossip – *exaggerated* gossip – concerning my possible relationship between the master of Falk and myself had spread in the village.

'A fine looking gentleman, Mr Justin is,' she said ponderingly one morning, 't'would be better for him if he did have a proper wife by his side, though, to spend his days with. Lonely for a man without a woman, and since that last business,' she shook her head mournfully. 'Dear me! What he must have gone through—'

She broke off expecting and hoping for me to enquire exactly what 'that last business' meant – the smuggling raid or something else. But although I'd have liked to know the answer I was determined to show no interest in Justin at all. So I simply said, 'Life can be very difficult for many of us. But I'm sure Mr Llarne manages his own affairs very well.'

'Hm.' She was obviously disappointed and slightly

ruffled. But I'd said sufficient to end the topic, and for the next few days his name was not mentioned. I was out of The Goat and Flag more than I was in.

Then, quite unpredictably, there was a storm.

The morning was calm, mild, and comparatively windless with heaviness in the air, and a sullen line of cloud hovering on the horoizon of land and sea against a yellowish sky. I had a meeting with the solicitor at eleven o'clock, and after the midday meal went out for my afternoon walk earlier than usual, feeling an over-whelming need of fresh air.

I slipped out unknown to anyone at The Goat and Flag, and this time avoided the direction of Carnwikken. There was no one working there on that particular day, and the thought of entering the gloomy interior without human company of any kind was somehow depressing. So instead I took the path which eventually led to the lane that wound ribbon-like towards the distant line of tumpy hills.

There was a sultry, earthy smell in the air heavy with the tang of gorse, dry heather and woodsmoke hanging in a grey cloud from a farmstead on the slopes ahead. I'd walked quite a way when the first drops of rain fell, followed shortly by a faraway rumble of thunder. A faint shiver of wind rustled the bracken and short turf by my feet, and I decided to turn back. When I reached the inn the spots had increased to a heavy patter and the wind was rising.

'You're only just in time,' mine host said as I passed the bar parlour. 'Reckon there's goin' to be a real soaker, with this gale blowin' up from the north. Master Llarne's just about had time to get back to Falk. He came lookin' f'r you. Thought you'd be here, so did I, the missus searched f'r you, but you weren't around.'

'Oh. When was that?'

'As I said – not more'n half an hour ago, maybe less.'

'Did he leave a message?'

'No – just p'raps he'd be lookin' in tomorrow.'

'Oh, well – thank you, Mr Baragwanath,' I said. 'I don't suppose he wanted to see me about anything important.'

I could guess what. Carnwikken, of course. He was annoyed about not being given an answer yet concerning the sale of the house.

I went upstairs to my room and took off my cape, shook it, and found it was already very damp. The rain outside was increasing steadily, and the intermittent rolls of thunder were growing far more frequent between flashes of forked and sheet lightning. There was something unusually ominous about the atmosphere; as the wind gathered force flinging its fury of rain against windows and walls of the hostelry my nerves tautened. I felt suddenly alone again, a minute human being marooned in a puny shelter against avaricious and destructive elements, although the clink of glasses and murmur of male voices came from below. Soon my evening meal would be ready, the bar would be open for regular clients, farmers and fishermen mostly, and the rage of the storm would be over.

But it wasn't.

It was far worse. The storm intensified.

There was a moaning, a roaring and rushing sound as

though all the underground streams had burst into a torrent, tearing stones and granite from their bed, swirling from the moor above to join the relentless sea and raging wind in a fury of destruction.

The earth itself to my heightened imagination seemed to shudder and crack, but the final shock came when a window at The Goat and Flag shattered simultaneously with a heave of the ground and a blast of sound that sent crockery and glasses flying.

'Something's happened down there,' Mr Baragwanath gasped with his gaze to the east. 'Something Carnwikken way.'

'Oh, my Gawd!' a woman at the bar cried. 'There's an earthquake! God save us. And my Billy out fishin'. I told 'en – I told 'en the weather wasn't right. I *knowed*.' She staggered with a hand to her breast towards the door.

'Come back, Dolly,' a man said, taking her arm. 'You'll do no good out there 'cept drown y'rself.'

The woman muttered something and staggered back. Everyone was on edge.

I wondered about Falk and what Justin was doing. Falk was in a precarious position on its point of rugged land; but it was not Falk I need have wondered about.

It was Carnwikken.

In the early morning when the weather had at last settled into a mere dreary drizzle it was discovered that the ground below the court on the sea side of the house had collapsed and taken a piece of coast with it, including a wall and portion of Carnwikken itself, leaving only a heap of tumbled granite and brick in a mound of useless rubble.

The other side of the house facing the moor was intact. The gargoyles still leered malevolently from the porch and half the interior of the building had survived. I wondered about the vaults, and if any of the treasures Justin had alluded to were still there, but was warned to stay away from the property for the present in case of any further landslides.

I expected Justin to call and see me that day.

But he didn't.

And in the evening I knew why.

Joel arrived at the inn and told me Justin had thought he might find me at Carnwikken as I'd not been at the inn when he'd called in the late afternoon. He'd gone there and been caught on the fringe of the landslide by falling rock, and was left lying there hurt, unable to extricate himself through the whole of the night.

'I went lookin' f'r him when first light come by morning,' Joel said. 'A great gash on the head he had – all blood – you never saw such a sight, an' one leg broke. So I got help soon as possible from Billy Peters, the lifeboatman, and we freed him and managed to get 'en back to Falk. Then soon as possible I rode to get the apothecary from near Truro. He was all f'r sendin' the master to the hospital place but he wouldn' go. So he put the leg in a kind of splint thing – isn't that what they call it? – an' tended the cut. But it's my belief he has a fever. I'm tellin' you because I reckon he thinks a deal of you. But he doesn't know I've come and it wouldn't be any good you callin' because he wouldn' see you.'

I believe I said automatically 'But there's something I might be able to do'. I'm not sure. I felt numbed – incoherent with shock.

But I do recall clearly Joel saying bluntly, 'The master wants no one round but me – you tek my word for et, Mistress Teale, he wants leavin' alone. I'll keep you informed if anythin' happens. You've my word for et.'

And with that he turned sharply, and with his head thrust forward strode through the door taking the short cut to Falk.

8

News of Mr Llarne's accident quickly spread through the village. I was tempted to ignore Joel's command not to visit Falk, but decided it would be no use going immediately, knowing I'd be prevented from having any contact with Justin for the present.

A local girl who worked there for two hours in the mornings brought daily reports about the 'poor gentleman' who was, she said, 'A terrible sight with his face half gone an' one leg all smashed to almost nothen.'

I forced myself not to believe either wild description. The thought of Justin's suffering and the mental picture of his ruggedly handsome features cut and distorted was almost unendurable; but one day when the apothecary called at the Goat and Flag he assured me the fever was abating, the damaged leg would mend, and to a certain extent the cuts and abrasions with care and treatment would be mostly erased.

'The gentleman's strong,' he said, 'a fighter and a sturdy character. After an accident like that there's bound to be shock for a time, but he'll recover, Miss Teale, don't you worry. I know you're a friend of his, but leave him to himself for a bit, that's my advice.'

So I did.

The whirl of unreality in which I seemed to have lived during the last months intensified. Surveyors came to discuss the damage to Carnwikken, and an architect was of the opinion that almost two-thirds of the house could be made safely habitable. I, now being owner of the property, was in the legal position of claiming financial compensation. It was all bewildering to me, and I left the whole business completely in the hands of the solicitors.

There was of course no longer any courtyard. The coastline of the district was completely altered, and the only way to the back was from the side of the house which joined the gargoyled path cutting from there at a right angle through rough undergrowth down towards the shore nearer Falk.

Many times I started off on the way there, thinking that by chance I might catch a glimpse or have news of Justin, but always I turned back realizing that any contact with him would probably meet with a rebuff. Eventually I decided to write a letter. He might answer, if he was well enough, or merely tear it up. Whichever it was, he'd know how I felt. Worry for him had killed any remaining bitterness in me for the past.

It wasn't a matter for forgiving. He'd done much to help me escape from the Trevanions' clutches, and the thing between us was surely stronger than any mistaken ideas of right or wrong, blame or any lingering desire for revenge from me.

So one afternoon I got pen and ink and started a note.

Dear Justin,

I was so very sorry to hear what had happened to you, please believe that – but I'm not going to show too much pity because you'd hate it, and you don't need it, you're such a strong person, and I know you'll get over it like you have those other things you've mentioned to me but have never spoken about or explained.

Can I come and see you? I would have done before, but Joel pointed out you wouldn't want it. Still, I could tell you things about Carnwikken and what's being done to it. It will be much smaller when the builders and all the men – carpenters, etc. – are finished.

Please write or send word either by Joel or the girl to say whether I can come or not. I hope it's yes.

As ever,

Isabella or Kim, just which you prefer.

For three days I waited. Then the answer came.

Don't come. I do not wish to see you.
Justin

The long grey autumn turned to a cold winter approaching Christmas, and I was still at the Goat and Flag.

Most of the restorations had been completed at

Carnwikken, although some had to be left to better weather in the early spring. But I could not tear myself away. The knowledge of Justin cocooned as an invalid in Falk was like a magnet rooting me to the vicinity. Reason dictated that I was obviously unwanted, and was humiliating myself in trying to enforce my presence in his life. The dignified thing to do was to leave Cornwall immediately for some destination near my old home. From there my affairs and the estate's could be finalized leaving me free to make further plans. I could go abroad for a bit – somewhere on the Continent, France or Italy. My mother, although of humble birth, had been a self-taught, cultured woman; I remembered her telling me of artists – Titian, Turner, Sir Joshua Reynolds and others – and of course writers like Shelley, Byron and the Brontës. There were famous buildings to visit in Greece and wonderful monasteries and exotic vistas in Spain. Concerts to attend of fine music. Oh! – I would be rich enough to make my own choice. The solicitors had assured me of that. I ought to be thrilled at the idea.

I could have been under different circumstances.

But I wasn't. Simply because of Justin. He counted all that much to me. And the knowledge was almost frightening. He *shouldn't* – he shouldn't, not so much, I told myself desperately.

But he did.

And that was the truth. I wished at times I was a light woman – one of those he'd once referred to, who could squander herself for a night, then go away uncaringly, content to have been used. But we hadn't been like that – the thing between us had been beautiful, I told myself bitterly remembering the night of the drug raid. We had *loved* each other; truly. And yet I knew if I defied him now and appeared at the door of Falk he'd shut it in my face. He'd meant what he said in that cruel cold note. And why? *Why?* Was it something to do with the shattered portrait of the woman in the cave? Perhaps.

I just had to know; perhaps it was because of his injuries. Perhaps that's why he wouldn't see me. But once he met me face to face and knew any disfigurement didn't matter to me so long as he cared, he'd relent, and take me into his arms again. Then the worst pain – the pain of separation would be over.

The only other alternative – that he could have used me merely as an escape to brief forgetfulness of something or someone else, and that his frequent blunt threats and jibes had been the real Justin, was just unthinkable and I wouldn't consider it.

So something had to be done.

What?

It was at that moment I began to make plans.

On a quiet early evening in November, when thin mist blurred the landscape and sea beyond, I set off wearing my thick cape pulled closely round me, taking the lane to Falk. I'd heard that Justin was now comparatively active about the house, and I also knew that Joel had gone off to Truro on some business of his own and was staying away for the night. The daily girl had returned to the village following her two hours of work. Justin therefore should be alone.

I knew I was taking an outrageous risk in what I was

about to do, but I could no longer spend my life secretly fretting, doubting and worrying.

If this wild enterprise of mine resulted in failure I would leave Cornwall for good the next day.

There appeared to be no one about anywhere when I reached my destination. The side door of the house was slightly ajar when I arrived, so I pushed it gently and went in cautiously, pausing briefly inside the passage, watching and listening. A few steps led upwards to a flagged corridor on the ground floor. Ahead somewhere, the sound of uncertain footsteps, accompanied by the tap of what I took to be a stick, echoed through the damp air. That must be Justin, I thought, and I hesitated, senses tense, recalling those hollow echoes on the terrible night of the Preventatives' attack. When the sounds had faded I steeled myself to mount the steps and, keeping close to a wall, edged slowly and softly through the shadowed half-light until I reached a point from where the kitchen quarters and the front portion of the house were divided. A beam of light crept mistily across the floor. With my heart palpitating heavily I stood quite still again, hunched in an alcove, to be sure I took the right direction from there, and that Justin was not likely to bump into me. I unlaced and removed my boots, then stiffened, waiting. From certain sounds, and a flicker of light and shade to my right, I judged Justin to be in the kitchen, so I went in the opposite direction. Miraculously I found the main staircase, and softly as a cat on the prowl, went up and reached the wide landing where I knew his bedroom to be.

The rest was simple.

The inside was untidy. And I recall thinking with a stab of feminine domesticity momentarily piercing the sense of drama and tension – that men really weren't much good at looking after themselves, although I'd imagined Joel would do better for his master. But probably Justin didn't care about such matters except his personal appearance.

Justin.

The recollection of my purpose in his private premises drove me to quick action.

I pulled off my cape hastily and flung it over a chair, then went to the bed and tugged the quilt. The sheets were rumpled but clean. I turned and faced myself through the mirror.

I was wearing a pale-blue silk tea gown over fine lawn embroidered underwear that I'd purchased in Truro the previous week for this special occasion. Twilight was already falling outside, and a pale moon was mounting the sky. Very deliberately I unfastened the neck buttoning and took the pins from my hair letting the fair masses fall to my shoulders. The shadowed background gave added pallor to the figure facing me. It was me, and yet someone else besides – an ethereal-looking temptress of ghostly appearance waiting to ensnare a lover. Elusive, and – yes, beautiful.

Perhaps at that moment I should have been ashamed; my mother, I know, would have utterly condemned; but *would* she? After all, I knew nothing of her social life with the man who'd been my father until his death. The emotion that drew them together in the first place against family disapproval must have been intense. She must have loved him deeply. As intense perhaps as what I now felt for Justin.

And this was my life.

So much depended now on the result of my wild actions. My whole future.

I stood there for some time in a half daze, then presently turned and climbed into the large bed where I huddled down into the sheets, and drew the bedclothes up to my chin.

The sheets felt chilly at first; how long, I wondered, would I have to wait? And suppose he decided not to sleep here, but spend the night by the kitchen fire? The possibility was a grim one because in that case I'd have to trail downstairs in the early hours of dawn or before perhaps, looking like some phantom vision of an ancestral ghost.

The idea would have been mildly comical if it had not involved so much.

Whether I dozed or not during that period of waiting I don't know. But at last – at *last* I was alerted by a jerk of my heart when the sound of footsteps – a halting, uneven tread – drew nearer and nearer and the door opened, sending a beam of light across the floor. I lay motionless as Justin came in.

He was holding a lantern that sent a swinging light across the floor. The mellow gleam lit his face to brief clarity, throwing up the strong lines of features and jaw, accentuating the cruel scar marring the left side of his countenance. He shut the door automatically, then came forward, one hand grasping a stick to ease his limp.

I still didn't move, and at first he didn't see the hump on the bed. When he did his head jerked forward and after a moment – a moment of shock, obviously – he straightened up, staring.

'Who's that?' he shouted. 'Who the devil are you? Get up before I kick you out.'

He came forward, and I sat up.

'Hello, Justin,' I said.

His mouth half fell open. I tried to speak again, but couldn't. A lump had risen in my throat that threatened to choke me.

I was suddenly frightened, he looked so angry. The blue silk tea gown was no comfort. I knew he thought I'd done a dreadful thing.

'Get up,' he told me, and his voice was hard, ruthless. 'Do you hear? – you minx.'

I put one leg out gingerly, then the other, stood up and shook the blue silk to my toes. Then I smoothed the hair from my eyes and passed thick strands of it back over my shoulders.

He glowered.

'If you were a year or two younger I'd know how to deal with you,' he said, 'despite the wreck that I look. But you're not, are you, Isabella? You're a calculating, stubborn young woman who means to get her own way at any cost. And I haven't the mind or energy at the moment to waste words in argument.' He paused before continuing, 'So kindly cover your delightful presence with that odious sack affair and – *get out*.'

I didn't move; just stared at him unblinkingly and replied, 'No, Justin. You've told me many times to do that and generally I have. But this time's different. I've taken a lot of trouble to arrange things and get here. And don't forget how I've fitted in with you before, like letting you cut my hair, and pretending to be your wife.' He lifted his hand in a gesture of negation, but I took no notice. 'No. I *won't* stop. I've come for one reason – because you're hurt, and I believe you love me as I love you. I still do—' Suddenly this courage in me faded, leaving me weakened, wondering if I'd made a mistake and appeared stupid and vulnerable to him, just a silly, sentimental girl out to catch the first man who'd ever noticed her. He appeared so rigid and determined – so essentially 'male'. Many women must have trailed after him.

I moved away.

'All right. I'll go. But I'll never forgive you.'

I took my cape from the chair and was about to turn when I felt a hand on my shoulder.

'Isabella—'

I glanced back at him. The frown had gone, but his glance was unfathomable, with a wary glint in his eyes, 'Don't play the coquette with me, Isabella,' he said in hard level tones. 'What kind of a fool do you take me for? *Love*?' A derisive laugh, more of a cough, came from his throat. 'What sort of love could you expect from a man like me? Bitter, disillusioned – a freak with a crippled body and twisted mind. Well, let me spell it out for you. Nothing but humiliation. I should probably beat you, then despise you for your subjugation. Do you understand now? *Do* you? You should. You should have heard enough.'

He came a step nearer; but I didn't move. In those long moments of confrontation and tension beween us I noted many things about him that hadn't registered before. The flickering of a nerve near one temple – the varying flashes of emotions lighting his eyes, the sensitive upward curve of his lips in a small half-moon shape when they were still, and the wince of pain that crossed his face when a muscle jerked his arm that had been wounded. A hand was clenched on his stick, and the knuckles were almost as white as the ivory head. His manner was frightening; I knew with a faint inward shudder of fear, that he meant what he said.

I knew also that this man and no other was the only one I wanted, just as I knew there was another Justin of warmth and passion and ultimate compassion waiting to be woken. While we both lived I would never be free of him.

Never.

So we stood silently, waiting – for what? How could either of us guess? Until I heard him speak again still in those dangerous level tones. 'Don't defy me, Isabella. Get out of here while you can. Or by God I'll make you.'

It was then I threw back my head and wrenched the blue silk at my neck, letting the frilly thing fall to my feet. I lifted my arms wide, and managed to say, 'You're right. I'm a – what did you call me? – a coquette, and a very wicked woman, I expect. But only for you, and I don't mind your fierce words or your scars or your threats or your past, or anything, but *you* – you, Justin.' The words left my lips in a torrent. I was nervous no longer. It was as though those few wild seconds of truth had crumbled the rift between us. Now he'd heard, everything would be solved.

He shook his head slowly and came close. He could kill me, I thought, not really believing it, and waited.

But the warmth of his body crushing me was life not death, bringing conciliation that was a cleansing flame to flesh and spirit. Until then, I felt I had never really lived.

I do not recall exactly what followed, except the tremendous joy of fulfilment followed by peace. Reality registered slowly like waking from a dream. I was seated, propped up by cushions, on a settee near the library fire with my head resting on Justin's shoulder.

I couldn't see his face, but his voice was husky when he spoke.

'You'd be able to write a book now,' he said. ' "How to tame a monster" – or perhaps it should be just "Resurrection". More dignified, and that's what's happened to me.'

There was no mockery any more. And no veiled threat. I disentangled myself and stared into his face. There was a wry little twist to his lips but his eyes were solemn and searching.

'Why were you – why did you act like that, Justin? At first, I mean when you knew – we both knew how things were. It was the same from the beginning wasn't it? *Wasn't* it?'

'Questions again? Always *questions*.'

'Yes. Lots and lots.' I pressed my cheek against his rough coat. I could feel a jerk of his arm, and a twitch of his thigh, the bad leg.

'Oh, I'm sorry. You're in pain.'

'Yes,' he answered abruptly, 'and it doesn't help having a volley of words shot at me.'

'Can't you answer me – even now?'

'I suppose I owe it to you,' he sighed. 'It's a long story,

and it can only have one end, Isabella. So long as you accept that, you shall have the whole of it.'

I regarded him with a faint doubt gnawing me again. 'I'm not sure. The end is up to the two of us now, isn't it?'

He eased himself completely free of me and stood up. 'No, darling. A life together – which I presume is your idea – with my existence as an object of pity from a wealthy young woman, would be impossible – for me. I could never be that kind of milk-and-water husband. I have to take the *lead* – a man's role. This damned leg's never going to be right again. And you'd soon sicken of seeing this clown's face on the pillow when you woke up in the morning. The scar will fade a little, but not much. Don't you *understand*? Even yet?'

'Yes, I do. It's you who don't. You're making yourself a martyr. And why? Just vanity. You want me as much as I want you, but you're too proud to admit it or treat the leg and arm as just nuisances that need a little thought and care now and then.'

'Oh, Isabella.'

He bent down and kissed me; firmly on the lips. 'You're such a wilful – such a minx! And yet – I ache for you. Even now.'

'Then—'

'But it wouldn't do, my love. It wouldn't answer. I couldn't cope with a second time. The first was hell. But this—'

'The first?'

He grabbed his stick, walked away and stood staring out of the long window. Then he turned and limped back swiftly.

'Yes. The *first*. I had a wife; the one in the smashed portrait. *I* smashed it and had good reason to. She was a whore.'

A little shiver shuddered down my spine. His expression was so tense and hard, and except for the deepening red of the scar almost white with renewed bitterness.

'I suppose now I've started I should go on,' he added after a short pause.

So then I heard his story.

This I shall tell now in words as near as possible to his own.

He settled himself facing me, the fingers of one hand curled round a glass of whisky, and began.

'As a youth I was always a rebellious character with a streak of wildness in me,' he said, 'partly perhaps because my brother – he was four years older than me – fitted so perfectly into the image of what my father expected his heir to be. We were an old respected family, squires of the district with a flourishing estate to uphold. Leo, my sibling, read history at Oxford, returning with a First to Falk. It was expected of me to follow more or less in his footsteps, but the scholarly life bored me and I rebelled, so I landed in the navy. For eight years I sailed the seas, adventuring and exploring, and seeing the world. There was hardly a land I didn't know. I had a full taste of exotic pleasures and women. Then my brother died of a fever—' He broke off reflectively.

'Go on,' I said.

'My father sent for me then as his heir. There was no one else; my mother had died when I was born. So I returned to Cornwall, not cheerfully, but thinking to get a bit of the respect and affection from my sire that had been denied me when I was young. It wasn't much good. I did my best for a time, trying to interest myself in the lives of tenants and running the estate – Falk owned a good deal of land, and there was always some problem or other to deal with. But that won't interest you. Anyway, the upshot of it was that seafaring and adventure were too much in my blood by then to get rid of. I was bored. What would have happened if my father hadn't died suddenly of a stroke I don't know. But that's what happened.'

'Oh. I'm sorry.'

He waved a hand to silence me. 'Why? He was a tyrant, a hard man. Still, I'd respected him, and his going was a shock. But it left me free, and I decided I'd live my life as *I* wanted and prove to myself and the tenants and villagers – all the lot of them who'd touched their caps and kow-towed to the old squire and "Master Leo" – that I was as capable and as worthy a landlord – better maybe – than my sibling and father before me.

'For a time it seemed to work.

'My father had been on the mean side; *I* spent money on property, installing new roofs to homes, giving parties for tenants' children on feast days – doing a number of social rounds that before would have been considered extravagant. But then, probably an easy existence wasn't enough. The old lure of adventure and colour got a hold on me. I wanted something else – something to stimulate my life as a mere country gentleman. A wife. Oh, as I've said, I'd had women before; I was no monk. But this was different. A woman by my side fit to breed fine sons and enhance the name of Llarne. A woman of grace and beauty and culture, making me the envy of other men.' His gaze darkened; for a moment I had a glimpse of the old angry look. 'I thought I'd find her. At that time I used to make seasonal trips to London. I had an occasional gambling session, and was a guest frequently at fashionable parties. It was at one of those that I thought I'd found her. She was an elegant creature, beautiful and cultured in the arts, and professed a liking for country life. Oh, she was clever, an actress, and gave the impression of having been widely acclaimed. I'd no idea then of her impoverished financial state, and no one told me.

'I married her and brought her back here to Falk.

'For a time all seemed well. I desired and worshipped her as much as any man can any woman. And then—'

'Yes – go on.'

He appeared to be looking back into some dark nightmare of memory.

'She cuckolded me. Being a fine lady and running a stately home wasn't enough. She was bored. She met some fancy stranger at a ball in Truro and that's how it began. Well—' He gave his derisive laugh again. 'You don't need to know all the details. For a time I knew nothing about it. Oh, she was cunning, very cunning. However, the affair leaked out in the end, as these things generally do. And I saw red. I returned one evening from a day in Plymouth, thinking to catch them, but they'd already gone – taken a coach to Plymouth, he was a rich bastard and she was a very ambitious lady.' He broke off before continuing, 'If I could I might have killed him and her with him. But I didn't have to. The coach was involved in an accident and did the job for me.'

'How awful,' I said automatically.

'It was Nemesis. After that I just went to hell. There's a kiddleywink about two miles from here along the moor where many a shady deal's hatched. I knew the Trevanions and others of their ilk, and soon got involved with their dirty work. There was a certain challenge in defrauding the Revenue, and profitable gambling sessions. And women can go cheap there. I had no conscience any more. I'd been made a fool of – in future I'd do the fooling.

'So that, my dear Isabella, is how and why I went to hell.

'But with one mistake,' he added, 'Silas.

'Silas caught me out on a weak spot, my temper.

'One night there was a scene, a shooting over an unpaid debt – nothing to do with me, but I got involved. A Revenue man was on the scent there concerning certain smuggling business. Guns were fired in the confusion, and the man disappeared. It was thought he'd been murdered. Warrants were out and rewards appeared for information. It was then that Silas conceived the wily plan to embroil me.'

'How?'

'If I did not comply, by openly stating he'd seen me shoot the Preventive man and kick his body into the sea.'

'But he *hadn't* – how could he? and why?'

'He could and he did for the express purpose of using my terrain and co-operation for the landing of a large cargo of contraband including opium – a tremendously pricey and valuable product. It sounds like an adventurer's plot connived by an amateur schoolboy. But Silas was no amateur. And in spite of his devious sly ways he'd managed to be kept so far in good regard by the law.'

'So you mean – you mean you were blackmailed?'

'Yes. For a time. Track had been kept of the drug from India being despatched through the China Seas, to France and the Channel. But remember, I knew nothing of this; when I gave permission for my creek to be available, the cargo was said to be mainly a large one of brandy and silk. As soon as the truth registered I got on to the Revenue and Fitzgerald. Through *you*.'

A faint smile touched his lips. 'You, Kim. I was not going to see Falk or any girl debased by that filthy stuff. I still had a shred of decency left, and by then I'd heard also that the officer in the shooting affair was still very alive and kicking. His disappearance had been simply a ruse by the law to enable his secrecy over a certain other business. Well—!' Justin sagged back. 'That's about the gist of it.'

I felt in a daze; there were so many ends still to be tied up. And only one issue to me was important – my future with Justin. But suddenly the recklessness that had driven me to face him today had died into uncertainty. How could I possibly force him any further without appearing bold and bad mannered? Justin, angry and frightening, was one thing. Justin as he appeared at the moment – gentler, more reasoning quite a different matter. Confusion bordering on shyness swept over me. We did need each other passionately, deeply, I was sure of that. But perhaps he definitely didn't want real emotion any more. Perhaps he just wanted to live a man's life alone except for Joel, brooding and longing secretly for that other woman he'd admitted he'd worshipped until she let him down. I could imagine him kicking the portrait to bits and crunching it with his boot. But he hadn't thrown it to the tide when I saw it – he'd left it lying there so he could sneak a look at it and remember, when he felt like it.

For a moment I hated her.

'Well?' I heard Justin saying, 'what's niggling you? Is my story so shocking? I'd have thought it was the natural outcome of a disordered life.'

I pulled myself together. 'Shocking? Of course not. I'm sorry for you – I mean not *you* exactly, I know you don't want pity – but that things happened that way for you. With your wife.'

'Forget it. Obviously I'm not the type for matrimony. Anyway, now you're here we have other things to discuss, haven't we – the house, Carnwikken.'

Of course, I thought, it would be that. *I* didn't count at all, comparatively.

I thought for a moment, then said, 'I haven't any idea of prices for property – not yet, and – you haven't given me any idea of why you want it, Justin. Anyway, I wouldn't have thought it could appeal to you as it is now.'

He regarded me with the old stubborn stern look. 'It's not for you to have ideas about my intentions,' he remarked bluntly.

I flushed. 'You really can be quite – rude,' I said with a flash of temper.

He laughed, then unexpectedly thrust out his good arm, pulled me to him, and kissed me on the cheek.

'I don't go in for apologizing and pretty speeches, Isabella, especially to you, and I don't have to have reasons for things. Let's say I just *want* it.'

'As a possession?'

His brows lifted. 'There you go again. Yes, as a possession. Something Cornish, for the Cornish people, if you can understand a touch of philanthropy. Carnwikken's got a history. Even as it is, what remains of it, is interesting and not only to me. And I want to preserve it, just as your kinsman would have done if he'd kept his strength and sanity in the hands of those rogues.'

I said nothing, so he continued, 'In the future visitors will be coming to these parts, lured by its freedom and wildness and sense of adventure, and by something else – its ancient past. I've no mind to see old property like Jeremiah's – and he was a splendid old boy in his wicked way – given over to grasping money-makers from up-country wanting to get their hands on any available property to turn into boarding-houses and hotels.'

'Oh. I see. Just *that*.'

'No. Not just that.' Apparently forgetting his refusal to explain, he continued, 'A mile or two away along the coast, past the kiddleywink, the coastline's gradually changing. The sea's biting chunks of land away in parts, at others the sand's sweeping in. A certain amount of excavation's already started where there's reputed to be a buried village taken centuries ago. Relics have been found of pottery, bones, and ancient implements used for primitive farming. I've a few myself. Year by year there'll be more. And it seems to me Carnwikken would be a good place to start housing them.'

'Oh. You mean a sort of museum?'

'When I feel like it, yes. It all depends. *Now* do you see? Are you satisfied?'

'I'm trying to,' I said. 'But it's quite difficult to imagine you settling to anything so – so—'

'Limited and scholarly as curator?

'I didn't mean that.'

'I think you did, Isabella, and I may have no other choice. A middle-aged man – and I'm nearing forty – with a crippled leg and shady past. Oh, I'd still be capable to sail a brig, and tackle pirates in the China Seas. But I haven't the heart any more.' His face sobered. He was staring as though into a lost world, and my heart went out to him.

'Oh, Justin,' I said, with a return of my old recklessness. 'Of *course* you can have Carnwikken.' I broke off as all the muscles of his face softened and relaxed.

An arm went out to him.

'I love you, Justin.'

He shook his head slowly. 'And by God! – I love you too,' he said.

And that's how it happened.

9

I returned late at night to the Goat and Flag, following the passionate and wonderful episode with Justin. In spite of his injuries and sticks he insisted on seeing me up the lane to the top of the slope from where the inn lights spread a pattern of light, giving a side view of the porch.

'I shall watch until you disappear inside,' he said. 'So no other midnight larks.'

I threw him an anxious glance. 'You must be—'

'Don't say it – tired? Maybe I am. That's your fault.' His face was momentarily in shadow, so I couldn't see his expression, but I fancied he smiled.

Minutes later I was facing an indignant Mrs Baragwanath. 'It isn't like you to be so late,' she grumbled. 'Past twelve, and you wandering all alone about the moor. Or weren't you alone? Joe was wanting to lock up and said he thought he saw two figures by the bend down the lane there Falk way.'

'Quite true,' I answered. 'I had a business meeting with Mr Llarne – about Carnwikken.'

'Hm.' She turned away, not believing me of course. And

I was surprised how easily I could have thought to mask the truth.

Despite what had happened between us, Justin didn't broach the subject of marriage, and I remained silent, no longer able to face the thought of forcing myself upon him.

I just waited, telling myself that in the end he'd take the initiative – the feeling between us now would prove too strong to be rejected through any false sense of vanity on his part. His limp would not be so noticeable in time, and the facial disfigurement would lessen and could even add an extra touch of dramatic adventure to his appearance once the first deep scarring had faded.

An exhumation for the remains of Jeremiah Teale had been undertaken, and the following week an autopsy was held, resulting in the verdict of 'death from natural causes'.

My great uncle's body was taken to the local church for a funeral service and buried in the family grave there.

I shall never forget the occasion.

It was a grey day, with just a thin shaft of pale sunlight glinting behind silvered clouds. Snowdrops and a sprinkle of very early primroses starred the dark earth round the tall granite gravestone, and Justin held my left hand as we stood by the graveside.

Just one wreath, my own, of Christmas roses lay there on top of the coffin.

Before the coffin went down it was taken off and laid with the other wreaths heaped round. There were masses of flowers. Obviously my old relative – despite a history of smuggling, perhaps partly because of it – I'd learned by then that smuggling of certain commodities was almost a way of life in the district – had been a popular character.

A slight breeze rose and caught the thin black veil from my face as we turned and walked away.

Although I'd never known him, a threat of tears flooded my eyes. Tension, I supposed, tiredness, or just the inevitable sadness of mortality.

As though in compensation and a welcome to the future, Justin's hand pressed mine hard, and the firm warm grasp brought life to my heart.

And that night he asked me to be his wife.

On the evening following the funeral Justin and I took a walk to Carnwikken and stood at the top of the drive before continuing to the house. Twilight would soon be shrouding the moors and sea, and shadows filled the porch where the ancient gargoyles loomed grotesquely facing the grey sky.

I recalled my first glimpse those months ago when I'd thought to find my Uncle Jeremiah alive and reigning there, and although we'd never met a sense of loss rose in me, emphasized, of course, by the day's occasion.

'What's the matter?' I heard Justin saying. 'Regretting your decision, are you? You can keep the place if you want. Though architecturally it's an eyesore, and I certainly wouldn't want to think of my wife living there.'

At first the words didn't properly register then, with a shock I realized what he'd said, and my first thought was of the woman he'd told me of – the portrait in the cave.

'Your wife?' I asked stupidly.

'That's what I said.'

His arm went round my waist. I could feel a hand pressed against my ribs and breast then on my cheek and chin, turning my face up to his. The glance in his eyes was soft and ardent; despite the fading light I could discern the whimsical half-moon curve of his lips – lips that could be so stern sometimes – coming down gently to meet mine.

After the drawn-out sweetness of contact he said quietly, with such love in his voice I almost fainted, 'What did you expect, my sweet wild love? After all you've put me through, did you ever ever dream I'd let you escape now?'

'Oh, Justin,' I managed to say. 'I didn't know what to think. I wondered—'

'Shsh.' He silenced me with another embrace, then said a little more lightly, 'Surely you didn't expect me to propose, kneeling, like any normal conventional swain? I hardly could, without a decent knee to bend. In any case I'm not *asking* you, I'm telling you.'

I smiled.

And together, with his arm firmly round me, we went down the drive to Carnwikken.

And so my story had a happy ending; with a few clouds ahead too – but then true happiness must hold a little storm as well as sunshine, like a spring day, and when arguments arose between us Justin invariably won – or rather I let him believe he did.

The museum was founded, and gargoyles still guard the entrance to Carnwikken, as enduring and formidable as the Cornish granite of which they were hewn.

Gigantic tides still sweep the coast and the terrain they have claimed, like the buried village and the lost land of Lyonesse, that lie forever mysteriously hidden beneath the cliffs and dunes.